THE SACRED JEWEL

Books by Nancy Faulkner

The
Sacred
Jewel

NANCY FAULKNER

DOUBLEDAY & COMPANY, INC.

Garden City, New York

Library of Congress Catalog Card Number 61–9505
Copyright © 1961 by Anne I. Faulkner

Author's Note

SOME people even today believe that Christ spent the time of preparation for his earthly ministry in England.

According to this legend, Joseph of Arimathea was the uncle of the Virgin Mary. He was a tin merchant who made many trips to the tin mines of Cornwall. On one of these trips he brought with him the boy Jesus. When Jesus grew to manhood and knew what he must suffer, he remembered the quiet hills of Cornwall and the lowlands of Somersetshire, the Summerland, half-drowned by the incoming sea. And he returned there to prepare his mind and spirit for what he must do.

Those who believe this legend say that Jesus came to a place called, in the old language, Ynis Witrin or The Island of Glass, which is now known as Glastonbury. Here, on the firm ground above the tidal waters, at the foot of a steep-rising hill called the Tor, he built a wattle hut and lived at peace with his neighbors.

Those neighbors were a kindly people with many hand skills —lovers of life and color and beautiful things. They were Celtic folk, descended from the tall blond invaders who had crossed the English Channel nearly one thousand years earlier from the forests of Germany and France. They lived, surrounded by water, in villages built upon sunken platforms in the marshy lakes. Their chief men were the Druids, powerful priests who controlled religion and law and government. They passed on their knowledge and their power and their secret magic lore to

7

selected young men of the tribes of Britain, teaching in oak groves sacred to the sun god, the only god they worshiped. Though the Druids knew a form of writing, they did not use it to record their history or their laws or their beliefs or their magic. All these things were committed to memory by future priests and priestesses in thousands upon thousands of rhymed verses.

The Druids celebrated each year three great religious festivals. At the Winter Solstice (December 21) they cut the mistletoe sacred to the sun god. The Beltane (May 1) was a fire festival, a happy time, when new fires were lighted on the altars in the sacred groves and the young men and women danced the night through and leapt great leaps over blazing bonfires. The most sacred and solemn of all the ceremonies was kept at Stonehenge on midsummer's eve (June 24). Scholars have proved that the Druids did not build Stonehenge, which had stood for unknown centuries before the Druid power became great about 500 B.C. It is generally agreed now that they adapted to their uses the great circles of standing stones at Stonehenge and at Avebury, which they called The Great Hill.

The Sacred Jewel is a tale about the Druids and the people they served in A.D. 30, when Cymbeline, the first man to call himself King of the Britons, ruled the southeastern part of England.

8

THE SACRED JEWEL

The map of
BRAN'S
BRITAIN
A.D. 29

CYMRU
(WALES)

Carleon
(Usk)

To the region
of the summer
stars.
(The west.)

ESTUARY

Ynis Witrin
(Glastonbury)

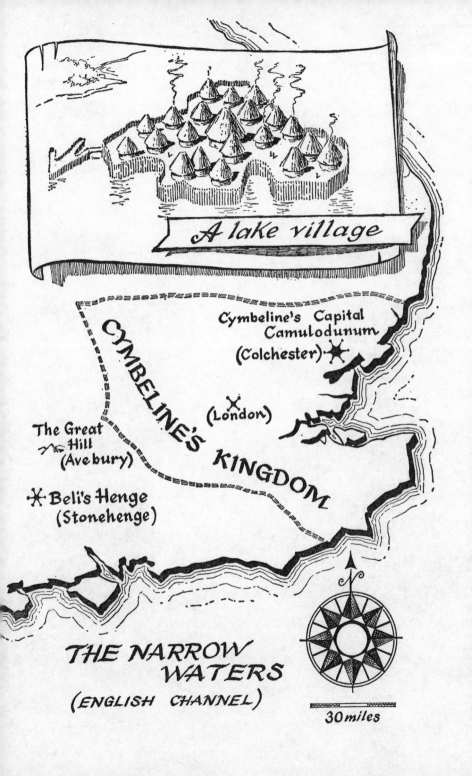

A lake village

Cymbeline's Capital
Camulodunum
(Colchester)

CYMBELINE'S
(London)

The Great
Hill
(Avebury)

KINGDOM

Beli's Henge
(Stonehenge)

THE NARROW
WATERS
(ENGLISH CHANNEL)

N

30 miles

CHAPTER ONE

"WHY doesn't he come, Carodoc? Three nights have passed since the end of the testing. He should have been here long ago." The girl turned from her loom with a gesture of impatience.

"Peace, Ysobel, peace," her brother said, laughing at her. "A woman grown you are. A woman, Ysobel, of full eighteen winters. Must you keep nattering like a child that will not wait for honey cakes? Bran the Brave will come when he will come—in his own good time and at the will of Abiris, our father."

Ysobel looked at him with irritated affection. He sat on a stone bench near the fire, one shoulder hunched a little, as it would be always from his old wound. He was a head span shorter than she, as dark as she was fair, opposing his slow, easygoing gentleness to her quicksilver impatience.

"Nattering am I?" she said. "How then would I not be nattering when my mind runs out to hear from Bran himself that he has passed the tests and my eyes stretch to see him in the blue robes of a bard?"

"Do you doubt he has fulfilled the requirements then?" Carodoc asked, teasing her. "I thought Bran was beyond failing anything in your thinking."

"And so he is," she said. "In my thinking and in truth. You well know he holds firm in his mind all the history of our people and the wisdom of the men of old. Twenty times a thousand verses he can repeat without halting, even under water."

"I do hope so." Carodoc spoke dryly. "Else he'll surely not be wearing the blue robe when next you see him, for every bard must do as much."

"Oh, *Carodoc!*" She stamped her foot on the hard clay floor. "You know he will. You know it. Our father says he's the best student in all the Druid colleges. Here *and* across the narrow water."

"Except Evelake," Carodoc said softly.

"Oh, Evelake, Evelake, Evelake. I'm weary of his very name, Carodoc. Evelake the Beautiful, Evelake the Wise, Evelake the Blessed. He cannot hold a rushlight to my Bran. He's a lazy, cruel—*beast,* is Evelake, for all his pretty face and quick wit. To hear you sing his praises, a person would think you'd made him as you make the bronze mirrors and shields on your forge."

Carodoc looked at her and smiled—a sad kind of smile— and lifted his hunched shoulder, not knowing he did so, and said nothing. At once she was beside him, her arm around him, ashamed of her outburst, remembering why Evelake was so dear to him.

She had not seen the accident that had cost Carodoc the free use of his throwing arm and ruined his hope that he would become the chief hunter of the tribe. She had been a small girl of seven summers and Carodoc a boy of twelve when it had happened. But she had heard the tale, she thought, a thousand times, and it rose now, clear in her mind. Carodoc had been on his first hunt with the men—proud of the strength of his throwing arm, which had that day sent a lance straight and hard into the heart of a boar; proud that the years of his boyhood spent in exercise and practice when the other boys were playing had made him the youngest hunter of the tribe a full two years before the usual time.

The hunt was over, and the men returning to the camp, singing and joking. Evelake, always spoiled by his parents, had been allowed to come to the camping place to watch the hunt from a safe distance with a trusted servant of his father, Ganhelon. Evelake, only eight—and willful even then —had run ahead of the servant, as he was not supposed to do, to meet the hunters. He had not seen the rush of a boar, which had escaped, with a sore wound, into the forest and was returning now, angered, to avenge himself upon those who had hurt him. The maddened creature had come straight at Evelake, and the hunters, held for a moment as statues by the horror of the scene, had not been able to move.

Except Carodoc.

In spite of his youth—even, Ysobel thought, with a flash of insight, because, being younger, his mind saw first the need of action and had no space for limb-binding fear—Carodoc had thrown his body between the charging boar and the boy, who was screaming with terror. Carodoc had had no spear to send at the creature. He had only his sword, which he had thrust ahead of him to the limit of his reach to turn the charge a little. Enough to save his own life and Evelake's. Not enough to save his spear arm. The wicked, sharp tusks of the boar had gone through his shoulder, tearing muscles that would never mend, ruining in one moment his chance to become chief of the huntsmen.

Another person, Ysobel thought as she knelt beside him, might have spent the rest of his life in bitterness and in hatred for the willful boy, whose disobedience had caused such destruction. Not Carodoc. Not her brother. He had,

15

when the long weeks of his recovering were done, accepted gladly the help of Rawn the Smith and learned the skills of working in iron and bronze and gold and silver. And he had become a second father to Evelake, spoiling him as much as his parents spoiled him, taking pride in his beauty and his brilliant, growing mind, willing to hear nothing against him.

"Forgive me, Carodoc," she said, the recollection of his bravery and gentleness making her humble.

He answered what was in her mind, as he so often did. "Little goose," he said, "do not waste your pity on me. It is better to be a maker of beautiful things than a hunter, for a hunter only destroys. Beli, God of Light, had me in his eye that day he set the mad boar charging."

"That may be," she said. But she thought it was Carodoc's own courage and patience—rather than the eye of Beli—that was responsible for his success as a maker of things which were so beautiful it almost hurt to look upon them. Quick anger against Evelake came up in her again and she added in a rush, "But Evelake is not worthy. He *is* lazy—and—and willful and I suspect he is cruel to the weak and the poor when no one is about."

Carodoc looked troubled for a moment. "Suspect," he said, "not know, Ysobel. The lad is young. And we have spoiled him—his mother and father and I. His life has been made, perhaps, too easy for him. But he will learn, my sister. He will grow in mind and in soul under the teaching of the priests. You will see."

She left him and went back to her loom, not trusting herself to speak further of Evelake, knowing her own dislike of him and, yes, even fear of some hidden thing she sensed beneath his beauty and his intelligence. After a moment, she said, "Come, look at the pattern and tell me if it is good."

got up lazily and came close to her beside the

standing loom and he examined the length of woolen cloth she was weaving. It was fine work, bright with squares of scarlet and blue accented with gold. "Yes," he said, "it is good. *I* think it is good—if my thinking has weight with you."

"None more so," she said, and hugged him. "Oh, *why* doesn't Bran come?"

She thrust her shuttle into the wool and went to stand in the doorway and looked over the village. Bran said there were few like it in all the land of Britain. It was built for safety against invaders in the very middle of lake and marsh, a league to the west of the island of Ynis Witrin, which some people called the Glass Isle and some the Place of Apples. Her father had told her how men in the olden times had felled great trees in the forest with their bronze axes and dragged the logs to the lake shore; how the carpenters and masons had laid the logs together, close-packed, one upon the other to a thickness of four feet, to make a platform, which they reinforced with clay and stones, brushwood and bracken, and sank into the lake as a foundation for the village. She wondered now, as she had so often wondered before, whether those fierce ancestors had fashioned tight, round houses like these the villagers lived in today or whether their ancient places had been simpler, ruder structures. They had made the village safe, protected it by water and a stout palisade— though, all thanks and all glory to Beli, no enemy had come in her lifetime nor were like to come.

The sun was low in the west and the surface of the lake shimmered with gold. Nothing moved upon the water except a pelican, flapping its huge wings in awkward rise to flight. Great, ugly creatures, she thought, but good for eating. She lifted her eyes to the cone-shaped hill in the distance, dark against the eastern sky.

"The Tor is beautiful at sunset," she said. She heard Carodoc suck in his breath and turned and saw that he had the first and little fingers of his right hand held straight before him in the sign against evil.

"Come away, Ysobel," he said. "The Tor is a place of dread, not safe to look upon."

She turned back to the door. "Are you afraid of the Tor, Carodoc?"

"Yes," he answered her softly. "Yes, I fear it. Who would not fear the entrance to the place of the dead?"

"I do not," she said.

"The more fool you. What if you should see Gwyn on his white horse and his red-eyed hellhounds running, running, to find some soul ripe for death? You'd fear it then!"

She thought for a moment. "Not I. Gwyn and his hellhounds are but messengers of the kind Avallach and the Tor but the gateway to the blessed land of Avalon, where souls live on forever in beauty, as the Druids teach us. The Tor is a gentle place, Carodoc, not dread."

"Talk," he said, relieved to speak again with the authority of his extra winters. "You do not know what you are saying."

"I *do* know," she said. "I went there once. Bran and I. Right up to the top. You—you can see the whole world from the top. Looking out from the Tor is not like looking out from any other hill. There is something about the way the sun shines through the air that changes the shape of things. The little, near hills—the small, friendly hills that cluster about it—seem to be great mountains, and the high mountains to the west look no bigger than molehills. Far off, the sea glimmers; and, in between, the bogs are golden where Beli sends his light to kiss the reeds; and, out beyond, the good, firm land rolls free and wide and full of mighty trees. You should climb the Tor, Carodoc, and know its beauty."

"You and Bran—you walked the Death Road! I—I cannot

18

believe it, Ysobel. I cannot believe you would be so foolish. You would not dare."

"It took no daring, Carodoc," she said gently, thinking, as she had often thought, how much he was their mother's son, with the dark old beliefs and fears of the ancient gods strong in him.

"When? When did you go?" His words came whispering to her.

"We went"—she counted on her fingers—"nearly seven moons ago—after the Beltane—to say farewell to Joshua ben Joseph and wish him well upon his journey home."

"Joshua ben Joseph?"

"The stranger from far eastern lands who lived awhile on Ynis Witrin. You must have seen him, Carodoc." She turned to look at him and found him frowning.

"Once," he said, "when he came to the village to ask the use of Rawn's lathe. This Joshua was a good carpenter. I did not know you knew him."

"A good carpenter," she repeated softly. "He was a good man."

Carodoc was silent. She thought he had little interest in the man who had been a sojourner for a time in their land. She wondered that none of them—not Abiris, her father, Master Druid; or Ganhelon, the wealthiest man of the tribe; or even Bran, except as she had spoken of it to him—had seen and felt the great strength and great gentleness and the power of the stranger among them. She had talked to him when she could, had taken him small gifts of cooked fowl and honey cakes and apples from the gnarled trees that grew in Ynis Witrin. She had loved to talk to the stranger—or, rather, to listen to his clear and beautiful voice speaking of peace and good will. He had said little of himself. Because she had asked him, he had told her courteously but briefly that he had been born in a small village in a land far to the eastward nearly thirty winters before and that he had learned the language of the Britons when, as a boy, he had come with his uncle, a tin merchant, to the mines of Cornwall. The fair land of Britain and the peaceful people who lived near the Tor had stayed in his memory and when he would find a place of quiet where he could prepare himself for some hard task he must perform he had journeyed the far way back. He had not named the task and she had not asked further. He had said he was just a carpenter, but she had thought of him as something other than a worker in wood, something different, something greater and more powerful.

She had taken Bran to see him once or twice, but Bran had seemed somehow troubled by this man from the east and had held himself apart from their talk. Bran had gone with her to the Tor out of his love for her, not out of interest in Joshua ben Joseph. Bran . . .

"You—went—to—Tor—top," Carodoc muttered, interrupting her memories. "You and Bran. No good will come of it, Ysobel. I say it to you—I, Carodoc, son of the ancient people. You were not wise."

"Do be quiet, Carodoc. I am a part of the ancient people as much as you, since our mother's blood runs as quick in me as in you. Yet I——"

"But," he interrupted her, with something of triumph in his voice, "you have not the power. Only I in our generation have the power."

"And much good it does you. You've never even used it. Have you, Carodoc? Have you?"

She could not resist the chance to taunt him about his power. She wasn't sure just what it was, though she did not doubt he had it. She had heard its story from her mother a hundred hundred times. It had lived on through no man remembered how many thousands of winters since her mother's people had been driven westward and westward till they came at last to the land of Cymru between the mountains and the sea and, at last, had been left in peace there by the invaders from across the narrow waters. Her mother had said that her people were the true Britons, small, dark, sturdy people who fought fiercely for their land—but uselessly— against the tall, red-bearded men from beyond the East Wind. Her mother's people had been forced from their homes: some of them had been enslaved by the conqueror and some of them had kept their freedom and in time mingled their blood with the blood of the conqueror. All of them had kept their small bodies and black hair and eyes and their hand skills and the power. And, in all these things, their mother had said, proudly, Carodoc was truly an ancient Briton.

Carodoc interrupted her thoughts. "It is forbidden. You know it is forbidden by the priests, Ysobel."

"Then how do you know you have it, my brother?"

He did not answer, and she thought very likely he had tested it at some time, perhaps on one of his solitary journeys beyond the far mountains and across the estuary to their mother's people. His silence held a disturbing quality and she wished she had not spoken as she had. She wondered why, loving her brother as she truly did, she was so ready to disturb the peace of his thoughts. She wondered if she were, in truth, a little afraid of the unknown places of his mind, of the wide differences between them. She remembered that Joshua ben Joseph had once said that where there was perfect love there could be no fear. She shook her head, as if to rid it of her thoughts, and stared again beyond the landing place and saw a boat cutting the lake that blazed now in red and green from the dying sun.

"Bran!" she cried. "He's coming!" and would have run from the house as she was, without her winter mantle, had not Carodoc folded it about her shoulders.

Her mind was full of Bran as she ran to meet him. He had been her companion for as long as she could remember. Abiris, her father, had brought him home one night in the dark moon of winter when he was but a scrap of a boy. He had been born in a distant place and his father had been sworn brother to Abiris. But Bran's father had died of a pox and his mother, knowing the sickness to be in her as well, had sent for Abiris, and he had gone on a two-day journey and found Bran's mother already dead and the child whimpering in the cold house. Abiris had wrapped Bran in a wolfskin and brought him home and made him a foster son. In time Abiris had taken him to the sacred grove so that he could become a priest and so be assured of food and clothing and a house for himself and his family even though he was a landless man.

And now—now he was coming to her and she was sure he would be wearing the bard's robe. Her heart sang with the knowledge that the love that had been growing between them for many winters would find its true end in their betrothal when spring would bring them again to the Beltane. They had both waited for this moment until they were weary with waiting, and now the waiting would end and Bran the Brave would take her to wife, for now, as a bard, he would have enough, and more than enough, to keep them both in comfort.

She caught the boat's prow as Bran swung it into the open space between the palisades that protected the village and tied the thong to the landing post. He wore the blue robe! He wore the blue robe of a bard! The last of the sun fell upon the clean, white strip of his scalp, where his head was tonsured from ear to ear across its top, as if Beli himself welcomed the new bard with his touch. She had no words, nor needed any, as he stepped from the boat and put his arms around her. His serious, fascinating face, all crooked and mismatched, lighted in response to the pride and love so plain upon her own. He held her, hard, for a moment and said "Ysobel!" as if it were a prayer of thanksgiving, and let her go, and she saw in the waning light that the brown eyes above the full red beard of his manhood were clouded with trouble.

They went up the cobbled street, hurrying in the crisp November air, to the warmth and light of the hearth fire. She chattered to him, asking of the testing and of her father, Abiris; chattered aimlessly to cover puzzlement and hurt at his silence.

He had passed the first of the three testings he must undergo before he became a Druid. She knew how he had worked. Knowledge was not something easily come by for him as it was for Evelake. For nine winters since, as a boy of ten, Abiris had taken him to the oak grove to begin the twenty years of study required for a Master Druid, Bran had disciplined his mind and his soul and his body as a good Druid must. He should, this day, have met her with happiness. They should be rejoicing together that he had completed the first lap on the road to his goal. They should be making plans for their marriage now that, as a bard, he was entitled to support from the tribe. Instead, except for that one cry of greeting, that one moment of embrace, he had not even looked at her, had kept his eyes upon the door of the house where Carodoc waited, and said no word.

They were almost to the door and she stilled her tongue, which wanted to cry out her questions to him. The village was empty except for wispy jets of vapor drifting from the smoke holes of all the houses. The place was so still Carodoc's words came clear and sharp though he had no more than breathed them in his anxiety.

"Where is Evelake?"

Bran lengthened his stride and, leaving her to come at her own pace, went ahead of her. His strong, compact body moved with swift grace. He was only of middle height, not tall like Evelake, but he seemed to tower above Carodoc. He caught Carodoc's arm below the elbow with his right hand in greeting and stood, not answering the question, looking down.

"Where is Evelake?" Carodoc asked again as Ysobel joined them.

"He," Bran began, and stopped and coughed, as if he would free his throat of some obstruction. "He—I do not know where he is."

"You must know. He is your friend." Carodoc spoke fiercely, as if he would force the knowledge upon Bran.

"Yet I do not know. Oh, Carodoc, he failed his testing. Evelake failed. Evelake the Wise. The best of us all. The leader. The one we all thought would, one day, be the very Arch Druid. *Evelake* failed the first testing. Oh, Carodoc!"

Ysobel felt as if a great wind had passed and, in passing, knocked her to the ground. Evelake! Evelake was the cause of Bran's wretchedness. She turned to watch the Tor, stark black now against the darkening blue sky, and to reassemble her face that it might not betray her disgust of Evelake when she would follow into the house, where Carodoc was already putting fire to the rushlights. For a moment she stood beating her hands softly together in anger that Bran's triumphant home-coming should be so ruined. Then she closed her eyes and said a prayer to Beli that he would give her understanding for the two blind, stupid men she loved—her gentle brother and Bran the Brave, whom she would one day marry.

CHAPTER TWO

SHE thought that some of the tension had gone out of the men with the need for such small, homely activities as replenishing the fire and lighting the rushes. Bran had hung his blue cloak upon a peg beside her father's saddle and he stood, dejected, near the fire.

"I'll fetch you a cup of mead, Bran. You look as if you need it," she said, and poured the sweet, strong liquid into a drinking horn. He thanked her, trying to smile and not doing it very well, and drank the mead and sat down on the bench.

"Come and sit down, Carodoc," she said, "and stop prowling about like a hunting wolf."

He did as she bade him and, after a moment, said, "Bran. Tell me."

"There's little to tell." He sounded tired, as if all the energy of his strong body had drained out of it. "Evelake was doing well, as we had expected. He had no trouble with writing and harping and singing." Bran tried again to smile, but succeeded only in grimacing. He went on slowly. "Then came the memory testing. Evelake stood tall and shining like —like Beli himself, I thought. The day was bright and the sun tangled in his hair until each strand shone like gold. I think there was no one of us watching but well nigh worshiped him as he spoke the triads in his clear, deep voice."

The fire shadows danced on Bran's face and transfigured it to near beauty and Ysobel caught her breath at the splendor in his eyes. She watched him lovingly as he sat remembering the look of Evelake's face and the sound of his voice in an oak grove on a sunlit morning.

"What then?" Carodoc asked, impatient at delay.

"He did not falter for a time and a time. He spoke the verses that tell the history of our people, without faltering, as if it were a pride and a glory to him. But when he came to the laws of the god and the priests he did falter. It was only a little hesitation at first, quickly recovered, scarcely noticed. He went on again for an hundred verses and one verse. And then, Carodoc, then his speaking grew slower and more slow and his voice went away to a strand of gold so thin it could barely be heard."

"Was that the end? Did the priests cast him out at once, without another chance?"

Bran shook his head. "You know better, Carodoc. He had three chances. No one could believe he was unready. He was ill, one said, and another thought he was overtired. There was, in the whole grove, no one who did not will his remembering. It made no difference. He had not the words in his head and heart. He could not go on. He failed in the testing, and no man ever had fairer chance."

He paused and his fine eyes held a troubled look and he spoke again so softly they could hardly hear him. "It almost seemed he did not *want* to remember the laws and the teachings."

"What did Evelake do?" Carodoc asked Bran.

"He stood and smiled. Just smiled, Carodoc. There were few of us left, for the Druids had waited until the end for

28

his last test and many of the new-made bards had gone to their houses. He looked at each of us and smiled and gave no sign that he had brought shame to himself and pain to his friends. He seemed—he seemed—almost proud, Carodoc, as if he had done a fine thing."

Carodoc nodded slowly. "He would want no pity. He would put on a proud face and smile though he lost the world. And then?"

"And then he turned and walked away and there was about him that which forbade any one of us to follow. We gave him time. We stood awhile in talk, but there was no heart in it, and one by one the others left until only Abiris and I were still there beneath the oaks. And Abiris said, 'Find him, Bran. Go after him and find him.' I went to Evelake's place and he was not there and I sought him for a day and a night and could not find him and I came, at last, home. But he is not here."

He looked at Ysobel and, she thought, really saw her for the first time since he had held her at the landing. The look seemed to beg her help, and she forgot her anger at Evelake and the thought that had been in her mind, the thought that Evelake had indeed deliberately failed so that he might be free of the obligation to high goodness and dedication to the people that had been always the duty and the privilege of the Druids.

She answered the look in words. "Do not be troubled for him, Bran. He has likely only gone to hunt or fish or visit his mother's people in Carleon. He will come back. And he will not suffer as some would, not as a landless man, for Ganhelon has many cattle and many fields—even silver coins."

Bran put his arm about her and pulled her close to him. "He is my friend. How can I not be troubled for him? But

29

you are right. He will not lack for the means of living. It is not that I fear, Ysobel. His feelings run deep, and I fear he is sorely shamed and hurt by his failure. I fear he may do himself an injury."

Not Evelake, she thought. He'll do nothing to hurt *himself*, though what he may do to any poor unfree man who comes his way I'd not promise. She felt the old anger and dislike rising in her and she did not speak, knowing this was not the time to say ill of him.

Carodoc agreed with Bran. "I think you are right, Bran. I think we must find him."

"Where can we look? He is not in any of the expected places. We cannot search all Britain."

"There will likely be no need for far searching. Did you look in Annwyn's hut?"

"Annwyn's hut!" Bran took his arm away from Ysobel so suddenly he nearly knocked her off the bench. "What would Evelake do in the company of an outcast? Evelake would not be friend to any man so careless of the will of the god that he failed to keep alive his fire. Annwyn—Annwyn is a——"

"Peace, Bran, peace. You are too harsh by half. Even Abiris—and there is none so zealous in protecting the Druid laws—even Abiris did not call down the curse upon Annwyn. The swineherd did not keep his fire alive. That is true. For such an offense any other would have been driven from the tribe with every man's hand against him. And this you well know, Bran. But Annwyn is only a poor weak-headed creature, not a deliberate blasphemer or evildoer. Evelake has befriended him, taken him food when he was hungry and castoff clothing for his crooked body. Annwyn dogs Evelake's very heels when he can. And would hide him if Evelake seeks a place to hide from those who have seen his failure."

Ysobel looked at Carodoc, unbelieving, amazed at his talk. She, too, had seen Annwyn following Evelake, and she thought the terror in the crooked man's eyes was plain for all to see. It was fear kept him at Evelake's side, not devotion. She wondered how Carodoc could be so blind, wondered if she should tell them what she had seen. She moved her shoulders in a helpless gesture. They would not listen. She was but a woman and they well knew her dislike of Evelake. If they could not see for themselves, they would not lightly believe her.

"Yet I do not think Evelake would seek Annwyn," Bran argued stubbornly.

Carodoc made no more comment. He stooped and tied the tops of his shoes more securely about his baggy plaid trousers and started for the door.

"Where are you going?" Ysobel asked, stupidly, for she knew well enough he was going to seek Evelake.

"To find him," Carodoc answered her. His face was set in grimness and he kept his eyes turned carefully away from Bran.

Bran drew in his breath in a long, tired sound. He is worn out, Ysobel thought, seeing the lines around his eyes, worn out with worry and searching. "I'll come with you," he said, and got up from the bench and took his blue cloak from the peg and went to the door.

Carodoc put his arm about Bran's shoulder, pitying his weariness but giving it no quarter. "Good. It may be we'll both be needed."

They moved quickly through the empty night to the landing and untied Bran's boat and sent it swiftly over the marshy lake, through the channels in the tall grasses, to the eastward shore. When they had landed, Bran said, "Do you lead," and he followed Carodoc in the darkness lit faintly by a young moon. He heard a horse stamping and felt his face brushed by the soft breath of the cattle as they passed through the grazing grounds of the tribe.

A great white shape loomed in the pale glow from the moon. Carodoc veered sharply to avoid the herd of sacred oxen and took the trail through the forest. The trees towered above them, branches so closely interlaced that no hint of the moon penetrated to the path. Bran stumbled against the bole of a beech and muttered as the bark scraped his hand. Carodoc broke the long silence. "Hold to me, Bran," he ordered, and waited until he felt the light pressure upon his shoulder and went on again, his lynx-sharp sight, inherited along with his other special power from his mother's people, penetrating the black dark as easily as if the sun were at the noonstead.

Acorns crunched and dead leaves rustled softly where their feet scuffed the earth in passing. In less than a quarter of an hour they saw a light ahead and, almost at once, the outlines of a dark shape, and knew they had come to the tumble-down hut of Annwyn, the swineherd.

Carodoc pushed against the door and it swung slowly open, creaking a little. The smell of the room—a sour smell of pigs and dirt and rotting food—rushed at them. A fire burned in the center of the tiny sod house. Otherwise, the bare space between the walls seemed empty.

"He is not here," Bran said, and was surprised at the hoarse whisper of his words. His tired body sagged against the door-frame, and he heard the rotten wood crack and straightened quickly.

"Annwyn," Carodoc called. "Are you here, Annwyn?" He jumped when an answer came from the other side of the fire. "He is not here. Go away. Whoever you are. Go away or may the Lord of Evil fly off with you."

Carodoc automatically made the sign against evil. Bran went into the room and around the fire, his shadow jumping crazily on damp, uneven walls. "Evelake," he said. "Evelake, my friend." And could say no more for pity.

Evelake lay upon the bare, stinking, earth floor. His bright hair was tangled and matted with dirt. His fine woolen shirt, which had been white, was stained and greasy. He had lost his shoes and his feet showed red and raw beneath his twisted green trousers. He stared at Bran and raised a drinking horn in mock salute.

Bran said "Evelake" again and felt Carodoc beside him and looked at him in despair and a kind of shame. Carodoc bent over the prone figure and said gently, "Can you get up, Evelake? We'll take you home."

Evelake answered slowly, taking great care with his words, "Ho for the lily-white boys, dressed all in green." He turned upon his face and raised himself upon his knees and then to his feet. He stood swaying a little, squinting one eye shut. "Not green, no," he said. "I do crave your pardons. Not green. Blue. Blue for bard. The green robe will come later, will it not, Bran, when you are a phil—a phil-is-i-pher"—he shook his head—"phil-*osopher*. And Carodoc. Good old Carodoc. He'll *never* wear a priestly robe, not blue or green or white, because he'll never be a Druid, not being of pure blood. Lucky Carodoc-who-might-have-been-a-hunter-but-for-that-bad-boy-Evelake. And Lucky Evelake. Lucky, lucky, lucky . . ."

His voice drained away and he wavered and would have fallen into the fire had not Carodoc put an arm around him.

"Peace, Evelake. Anyone can fail a test. Do you not——"

"Take your hands away from me, Carodoc!"

33

Carodoc's face crumpled into puzzled unhappiness. Evelake brushed awkwardly at his arm. "Take your hands away from me I say! I will no longer be your—your *slave* because you saved my life."

Carodoc dropped his arm and looked at it as if it were not a part of him. Evelake swayed again toward the fire and steadied himself and moved a little away from them. "Do you *dare* offer me pity?" he asked. "Do you think that I— Evelake the Wise—failed in memory because I did not know the silly rhyming laws they set me? I will tell you, Carodoc the Maker and Bran the Brave, I had no *mind* to pass the tests."

"Evelake!" Bran said sharply, and moved toward him. "You don't know what you're saying."

Evelake backed away, evading him. "No. *No*. Keep your distance, Bran the Brave. Keep your distance and hear me. Who would be a Druid—a sniveling, whining priest? Be good! Be kind! Keep your body strong and pure! Be continent in all things! Keep the laws! Serve the people! Do not bear arms! Teach the young men! Eat the bread of charity! That's not for me. Not for Evelake the Wise, the Beautiful, son of Ganhelon the Trader, heir to the greatest wealth in all the tribe. Me a Druid! Beli forbid!"

Carodoc said sternly, "Hush, Evelake. Do not blaspheme the god."

"Blaspheme! Do not blas——" He broke the word off and turned away from them and leaned his arms against the wall and put his head upon them and sobbed as if he were a small boy again.

Bran and Carodoc watched him, stunned at the sudden change in him. Bran thought, he is deeply hurt by his failure, more deeply than I had reckoned. He is trying to hide his shame even from himself. He felt a tearing pity

for his friend and went and laid his hand gently upon Evelake's shaking back, offering comfort. Evelake jerked away,
as if the hand had been flame, and whirled around, his back
to the wall, his arms outflung along the dripping sods.

"Keep away from me, Bran!" he said. "But for you, I
would this day wear the blue robe. It is *your* doing. Yours.
All of it."

Bran's lips gaped open in surprise and he smacked them
shut and his face turned red with anger. *"My* doing? Mine?
Have you lost your wits as well as your memory, Evelake?"

"Your doing. Yes." Evelake was shouting. "You, the darling of the Masters, the lily-white boy of Abiris. Do you
think I have not seen? Bran the Brave will be Arch Druid
some day. So says Abiris in his pride for all to hear. He has
chosen you—from the time you were a kin-shattered boy
without mother or father to care for you, landless, cattleless,
and he took you in and nurtured you, since his own son could
not walk in his steps. Only I was more clever. I was fairer,
wiser, better born than you for all you could count your
blood pure for the nine generations. I was more like to win
the election when the time should come. But Abiris would
not like that. Abiris could not have his precious Bran outrun
by a better man. One more chance, just one more, at the
testing and I should have remembered. But Abiris would
not have it. Abiris . . ."

I must stop him, Bran thought. I must not let him say
such words. He is crazed with his failure. He knows these
things are not true. It is his own shame, and the need to explain it makes him talk so.

"Evelake! Stop!"

Bran roared the words, putting behind them all the power
of his deep chest, trained to fill a forest with song. The roar

35

echoed in the tight, hot, evil-smelling room, but it might have been a whisper for all its effect upon Evelake.

"Abiris made all safe for his beloved Bran. Is that not enough, Bran? Is it not enough that your way to power is smoothed and made sure? Must you as well forbid Ysobel to see me, fearing she will turn from you if she is let to know me well? What ails you, Bran? Are you so afraid of your own weakness?"

Carodoc had been standing to one side in the shadows, watching Evelake as he would have watched a favorite hunting hound turned vicious. Now he moved suddenly and stood before Evelake and said, "Enough! You are drunken with shame and mead. Guard your tongue lest you find——"

Evelake struck his lame shoulder, which was still sensitive to sudden pain after eleven years. The blow was not a hard one, for Evelake was still unsteady, though he had worked off some of the effects of too much drink in angry words. But Carodoc, taken by surprise and pain, fell to the floor and lay there for a moment waiting for the sharpness of the hurt to pass. Bran, forgetting a bard was forbidden to harm any man in anger, started forward, his fists doubled, ready to return the blow Evelake had struck.

Carodoc, sensing the angry movement, opened his eyes and spoke, gasping a little, but with command. "No! Bran! You must not. You are a bard. And I am not seriously hurt. This pain will pass."

Bran dropped his hands and stepped back, fury still showing in his eyes. He bent over Carodoc and helped him gently to his feet. Carodoc stood, rubbing his shoulder, his eyes full of sorrow and doubt. Evelake shuffled his bare feet. Carodoc and Bran turned their backs upon him and Carodoc said woodenly, his voice flat and hard, "Come, Bran. There

36

is nothing we can do here. We'd best go home before the night is all spent."

They did not see the beginning of contrition that had been in Evelake's face turn hard again as they went from the hut. They returned to the lake as they had come, in silence.

Bran loosed the moorings and held the dugout steady for Carodoc to come into it and saw him shaken, his face riven with trouble and sorrow. Anger at Evelake, who above all men had most cause to love Carodoc, swelled in his mind and, for the first time, a hair's breadth of suspicion of his friend's goodness came to disturb him.

He stepped into the boat and pushed it away from the bank and pushed the doubt from his mind. Evelake was not evil. He was but shamed beyond bearing at his failure and he had struck out wildly in his hurt. They had been friends for more years than he could count on his fingers. Bran and Evelake. They had wandered the fields and woods together and had studied together in the grove near Ynis Witrin, learning to sing and play the harp, learning the rhymed story and laws of their people. Together they had taken their great bows and iron-tipped arrows to the shooting ground and trained hand and eye to strength and accuracy far beyond the skill of other boys in the tribe. Bran thought he knew the heart and mind of Evelake and knew them to be as clean and clear and golden as the water in the two-chambered Druid's well when the sun was directly above it.

He dug his paddle deep into the water, as if he would beat down an enemy. There was no evil in his friend. He could swear to it. This—this appearance of evil was but a momentary thing. It would pass and be forgotten.

The boat slid to the landing stage at the village and Bran

caught the drooping branches of a young willow to hold the prow steady for Carodoc. Carodoc did not move from his seat. The setting moon was full upon his face and Bran saw the look of sorrow had gone and wondered what thoughts had been Carodoc's on the short crossing. Generous ones, Bran was sure, for there was no one so large-minded as Carodoc, so slow to think evil, so quick to forgive. He seemed at peace again and Bran was glad.

"Bran," Carodoc said softly, "let us say no word of this to my sister." He smiled a little. "For her own woman's reasons she thinks already of Evelake without kindness."

Bran nodded, seeing his fiery, stubborn, beautiful love, with her auburn hair flying above her gray-blue eyes, dark and stormy with sudden anger against injustice and cruelty —seeing her as clearly as if she were beside him and knowing gladness in thinking of her and of their coming betrothal. "Agreed," he said, and answered Carodoc's smile. After a moment, he added, "I do not know why she so mislikes Evelake. Beli knows it is none of my doing. But you are right, Carodoc. We'd best say to her only that we found him and he is safe in Annwyn's hut."

CHAPTER THREE

Ysobel pressed her amber ring into the damp clay and put the pot, with half a dozen others, beside the fire to bake. She stretched to get the kinks out of her back and fingers and stood looking at her work. They were fine pots, smooth and even in line and pleasing to the eye. She liked this last design.

She'd take it out to the forge and show it to Carodoc. He would be pleased, and it could dry as well beside his work fire as by the fire on the hearthstone. The flames were equally sacred, for both had been blessed last spring at the Beltane.

She picked up the torque she'd laid aside while she was making the pots. The great collar of bronze, enameled in rich, dark red and blue the color of a summer sky at midday, was a nuisance when you were working. She adjusted it exactly at the shoulders and tightened the matching belt so that her green and gold tunic fell more gracefully to her ankles. She threw her cape about her shoulders and picked up the pot carefully and went across the cobbled alleyway to the workshop.

She wished Bran would come. She was always restless and a little bored when she could not see him and talk to him, and he had been gone half a moon since the night he and Carodoc had sought Evelake. They had told her only they'd found him at Annwyn's hut, but she had not believed this was all they could have told. Something had happened that night, something unpleasant. She was sure of it. Bran had left early the next morning, before daybreak, while she was still asleep in her corner of the house. She had had no chance to question him, and you had as well question the lake as Carodoc when he chose to keep his mind hidden. But there had been a kind of uneasiness about her brother. His face, when she watched him, and he not knowing, had been deeply sad since that night, and he touched his bad shoulder often, not as if it pained him, but as if it carried an answer to something that puzzled him—as if it were a talisman that, touched often enough, would solve the puzzle.

She frowned a little as she stood before the door of the forge. She did want to know the whole truth of their finding Evelake. But she'd as well give over thinking about it. She would discover it in time. One or the other of them would tell her, lightly, as a tale long past, or in a troubled way, to share a thought too burdensome to be carried longer alone. Still she wished her mother had not gone to the place of the happy dead. Her calm, gentle mother, so full of the wisdom of the ancient people, would have known by magic what had happened.

As she stood with her hand upon the latch, Ysobel was swept with sadness and desolation and loneliness. It was hard being a Druid's daughter. People respected the priests, looked up to them, venerated them, sometimes loved them a little if they were kind in their dealings, as Abiris, her father, was kind. But the people were also a little afraid of them and did not come idly visiting the Druid's house as they did the other houses in the village. It had been many years since the young women of the tribe had made a friend of the Druid's daughter.

"Stop it, Ysobel," she said half aloud to herself. "Stop thinking like a witless child. You would not have it otherwise, for if it were otherwise you would not have Carodoc for brother and, likely, not Bran for your promised man." She looked at the pot in her hand, lifted her lips into a smile, and opened the door to the forge.

Carodoc was bent over his anvil, so absorbed in the sword he was finishing he had not heard the opening door. She watched him without speaking, proud of the skill in his long, deft fingers, thinking that whatever other forbidden power he might possess, there was a sure and present magic in his hands and head, a magic to draw living beauty from dead metals. He lifted the great sword in his two hands and ran his eye along its length, testing its balance and weight and the straightness of its edge. Satisfied, he laid it on a stone bench and turned, stretching, as Ysobel had stretched earlier.

"Beli bless you, my sister," he said when he saw her standing inside the door. "Are you a witch that you come through closed doors as silent as the shadow of a leaf?"

"Do not jest at witches, Carodoc. You were so intent upon your work you did not hear the latch." She went to the bench and looked down at the sword. It was a beautiful thing, the hilt intricately worked into the semblance of a deer's head surrounded with mistletoe boughs and inlaid with gold. "Have you become swordmaker to the great Cymbeline, who calls himself King of the Britons?"

Carodoc shook his head, laughing with his eyes. "And how would Cymbeline, in his fine house on the eastern shore, know of the poor ironworker far beyond the stretch of even *his* power? No. The sword is for Evelake." His eyes stopped

41

laughing and the light went out of his face. "Poor Evelake. The gift may bring some easing to his sorrow at failing his tests."

Ysobel said, "Oh," and dared say no more, for fear she would lash out again at Evelake and anger her brother. She held out the pot for him to see. "Do you like it, Carodoc? See how the ring you made flows into the curves of the clay. Is it good?"

He took the pot from her and examined the design. "It is more than good, Ysobel. It—it is splendid. Shall I set it here beside the forge for drying?"

She nodded, feeling a little warmed by his praise, which he never gave idly. But the warmth did not quite reach the cold place in her heart, where there was still a remnant of the loneliness and despair she'd felt outside the door. She wandered about the small workshop, picked up the bellows and pointed it at the forge, and saw the gray ashes of the forge fire glow red. The quickened sparks reminded her of Joshua ben Joseph and his talk of man's spirit so easily quickened to fuller life by the power of love, and she felt comforted.

"You are troubled, Ysobel? What is it?"

"I wish I knew, Carodoc, my brother." She smiled at him, but it was a wry smile, with no merriment in it. She was not surprised at his question. He had always had the power to see inside her mind. "Perhaps it is only that Bran has been so long away. Perhaps—perhaps it is the talk of witchings whispered in the village. Have you heard it?"

"Yes. And I do not like it. It is, I think, or at least hope, no more than idle talk, but it is not good for such whisperings to be." He frowned and rubbed his shoulder in the asking way she had noticed.

"We've not been troubled with witches for many moons,"

she said. "And the whispers are vague, naming no one. Perhaps it *is* idle talk. But it disturbs me, too, Carodoc. Talk of witches and warlocks, especially so close to the dark time of winter, means . . ." She hesitated, trying to pull her thoughts into clear form. "It may mean that some one —some one of our people is bent upon mischief."

"Yes." His eyes found the sword he had made for Evelake and rested upon it.

He thinks of Evelake as the mischief-maker even as I do, Ysobel thought, and began to put her thought into words. "Do you suppose, Carodoc, that Evelake——"

But he cut her off. "I suppose the day is bright and warm for the time of the year. I suppose we have both been too long bending to work, you to your clay, I to my forge. I suppose I will put aside my apron and go with you out into Beli's sunshine and we will cleanse our minds of these dark things. Come." He held out his hand to her and they went forth together.

"Let us go to the oak grove, Carodoc. I've not been there since midsummer and it is ever a peaceful place."

They crossed the lake quickly, moored their dugout, and struck out in long, smooth strides, singing a hymn to Beli. They passed the fields of corn and barley, empty now, lying fallow, waiting for the spring sowing. They passed the herd of sacred oxen, slow-moving white humps against the autumn brown. Beyond the oxen they could see the horses. Ysobel broke off her singing to whistle a call and Caw, the dapple-gray gelding she'd raised from a colt, galloped across the field to nuzzle her shoulder.

Carodoc shouted and she saw he had already entered the grove of ancient oaks. She came up beside him and found him staring into one of the trees and pointing. She looked along his outstretched arm and saw what he saw

43

and cried out in joy, "The mistletoe! Beli has sent his thunderbolt to bring mistletoe to our own grove. Our tree is blessed, Carodoc, and we are blessed."

"Yes. It is a good sign, Ysobel. We must get word quickly to our father."

There was no joy in his words and she thought seeing the mistletoe had brought sadness to him. She guessed he was thinking of Evelake and wondering how, with the sign of the god's favor already among them, Evelake could have failed his testing. She wondered herself and, for a space, doubted again, as she had doubted before, the ancient lore of the god cherished by the priests. She found she was thinking again of Joshua ben Joseph. His faraway, eastern god—if she had understood him aright—ruled his people through the power of love and compassion without such magic properties as mistletoe and sacrificial oxen, and she thought, with a passion of wishing, of the comfort of such a god. She drove the thought from her, a little frightened by her sacrilege, glad her father could not know her traitor mind.

"Come, Ysobel. If we hurry I can leave you at the village and take the news of what we've found to our father before moonrise."

He scarcely gave her time to get out of the boat at the landing before he was off again, dipping the short paddles deep into the channel, sending the boat swiftly westward. She started slowly through the cobbled lanes of the village, thinking again of the ugly whispers of witchcraft. She had heard of no definite spells—no cattle with udders suddenly dry, no children stricken dumb and witless or men bereft of movement. It was only that recently, when she had come suddenly upon the villeins talking together, the talk ceased, but not before a whispered "witch" or "warlock" hung like an echo in the stillness. If there *were* witch-craft (she shivered at the possibility), it would have to be found out and the witch or warlock punished as all criminals were punished—for the good and safety of the tribe. But, she thought, people were too quick to believe in witchings and the punishment was a thing of terror. She could still see in her mind the last witch trial and its result—the old woman, who, they said, had charmed beasts to sickness, burned in the wicker cage with the spellbound animals and the rabbit that was her familiar spirit. The horror of that execution would, she thought, never leave her. She almost wished her father had not taught her, as he had taught Carodoc and Bran, to reason carefully, because it was such reasoning that made her wonder if all those accused of witchcraft and burned for it were guilty. It was not always possible, she thought, to tell whether a beast was ill of a spell or of neglect or a natural sickness. It was not . . .

"Ysobel! Wait a little."

The call came from the landing stage behind her and, without turning around, she knew it was Evelake who called and knew herself trapped. She could not pretend she had not heard him, for his rich, sweet voice was as clear and penetrating as a harpstring and trained to carry to hundreds of people. She had not seen him since long before his testing and she had no wish to see him now. Yet, because she was a little afraid of him, she did not want to anger him by walking away from his hail, and she stood in her tracks, waiting for him to come up to her.

"Beli bless you, Evelake." She gave him the customary greeting formally, without meaning it, when he was still five paces from her. She saw his face twist in mockery and straighten again in the blink of an eye and wondered whether his scorn was for her or the words. He came closer and stood looking down into her face, not speaking, studying her as if she were a morsel of honey cake he was considering eating.

His look made her uncomfortable and she turned quickly from him and started off again toward the haven of her own doorway, hoping he would know her discomfort and leave her. But he fell into step beside her and said, "I have missed you, Ysobel."

She spoke quickly to avoid more personal remarks. "I am sorry, Evelake, about the testing. It was bad fortune." She did not know the words fell cold and formal into the space between them. Because she was not looking at him, she did not see the anger leap in his eyes as the forge fire had leaped to the breath of the bellows. He said lightly, as if she had regretted a cloudy day, "It is nothing, Ysobel. I have no need to be a priest, being no landless, kin-shattered man."

She looked at him then, angered by his words, meant, she was sure, as a slur upon Bran. She was, indeed, for the moment, too angered to speak. If he noticed her fury, he gave no sign, and, before she could calm herself for words, he went on.

"My father is the wealthiest man in the tribe and some day I shall have all his wealth—and more, for I intend to make my own riches as well." He stopped, as if he waited for some comment from her, but she said nothing, wondering why he was boasting of Ganhelon's wealth. Surely he must know his father's land and cattle, hunting dogs and store of silver coins meant nothing to her. She wished he would go away.

"Some day, my sweet Ysobel, my love—maybe sooner than you think—I shall be ready to come for you to make you my true lady to share with me all that I have."

She looked at him stupidly, not for a moment understanding that he was asking her to be wife to him; not, when she did understand, believing her own ears. She stood beside him, her mouth a little open, her eyes clouded and round with disbelief. He chuckled, and the sound of his merriment had, to her, something dark and evil in it that roused her from stupefaction. She spoke so rapidly the words seemed to tumble from her mouth, forgetting to fear his anger in her eagerness to bring his talking to an end. "Are you bewitched, Evelake, that you speak to me of these things? You know I have been promised to Bran the Brave for as long as I can remember."

He threw back his head to laugh full and long and the laugh was an insulting thing. Her body was rigid, held tight against the insult, suffering the hideous sound, knowing it would do no good to protest. When he had had enough of his own amusement, he wiped his eyes with the back of his hand and said, "So good a jest, Ysobel. Promises are made to be broken, and who would be wife to the dull and ugly Bran, landless and kin-shattered, when she could be *my* lady? Am I not the most handsome man in the tribe and have I not but now told you of my wealth? Promised to Bran! Oh yes, the jest is good, my sweet."

She slapped his face and the laughter went away, leaving a look so wild and so full of evil she stepped away from him, shaking, and looked about the village, seeking someone to protect her, feeling sure he would strike her. There was no one in sight. Dusk was closing in and all the people were inside their houses. She looked toward her own house, feeling its safety reach out to her, knowing she could not get to it with Evelake barring her way. She gulped air, settled her feet more firmly on the cobbles, tightened her shoulders against the expected blow, looked— at last—into his face.

He was smiling.

47

Had she then imagined the hatred, the loathing she'd seen there a moment before? She knew she had not and wondered what manner of man this was who could put off evil as easily and quickly as a cloak, and feared him the more.

"Come, Ysobel. I will take you to your door."

She was trembling and she thought he knew it and took joy in her fright. He offered her his hand, but she pretended not to see it and gathered her cape close about her and walked beside him to the door, not speaking or trying to because she knew she could not.

She put her hand to the latch and he stayed her, speaking so softly she could barely hear him. He kept his head bent and she could not see his face. His voice was humble and the words he spoke were full of apology. "Will you favor me, Ysobel? Will you tell Carodoc I am fair shamed I struck him in Annwyn's hut? I—I cannot face him myself, so great is my shame."

"You—struck Carodoc?" she said. "You *struck* him?" A corner of her mind noted that she had been right in thinking something unpleasant had happened that night, but she had no time to consider it now. "You *should* be shamed." She wished she had better words to express her contempt of him, wished such words as she had were made of flame to sear him. "Is it not enough he is a cripple because of you? That he had to give up what he most wanted in his life because a silly, willful child would not obey his father? What has Carodoc ever done to you, since he gave you your life, except cherish you and love you, protect you and— and *spoil* you? You—you are vile, Evelake."

He felt his blood heated with anger and schooled his face that the fury would not show. Why did they all blame him for Carodoc's shoulder? Did they expect him to carry gratitude as a burden upon his shoulders for the rest of his life? Couldn't they know what it meant to be constantly reminded you owed your life to another man? He had thought Ysobel, at least, would understand and help him. His head ached and he hated them all. He didn't *want* to hate them. He wanted to go back to the old simple time before the testing when he was Evelake the Wise, Evelake the Beautiful, the darling of the tribe. Why couldn't Ysobel love him as he had loved her all his days?

He looked at her and knew his look was sullen and bitter and could not help it. "What do you know about it? Do you know the burden of being forever grateful to a man for the simple right to live? Yes, I hit him and I'm glad of it."

She stared into his face and she thought he winced before the scorn in her eyes. She lifted the latch and swung the door open behind her. He moved as if he would go into the house with her and she put up a hand to stop him. "Do not come near me, Evelake." There was in her voice a quality of command that reminded him of her father, Abiris, when he sat as judge in the courts. "Go away from this door. Go and think of the thing you have done to the heart of Carodoc, who has never asked you to be grateful—only kind and loving."

He made another move toward her and she went into the house and he heard the door rammed shut and the iron bar forced home to lock him out. He leaned against it and covered his head with his hands and would have wept, for he felt alone and an outcast because he had not been able to pass the stupid tests set by the Druids. He had failed and, in his failing, had lost the good will and admiration of the tribe. Every man's hand, he thought, was against him. He pulled himself straight. So be it. He would set his hand against every man and, most especially, against Bran the Brave, who had succeeded where he had failed.

He stood away from the doorframe and felt the cold probing beneath his warm mantle and snapped his fingers. As if the sound carried a signal to his brain, he took from beneath his cloak a strip of smooth bark and a knife. He spat upon the knife and drew on the bark the body of a man without a head. He worked quickly, sketching the flowing lines of a robe about the body.

As he cut, he whispered the name of each letter,

"C-U-R-S-E B-R-A-N." He looked long at the figure and the writing and shook his head and spoke softly to himself. "The old ones say such a curse will work its evil. It may be. It may be." He hid the thing beneath the house and turned and walked rapidly away. "If it does not," he said to the empty night, "if it does not, I, Evelake, will find some other way to have my revenge upon Bran the Brave."

CHAPTER FOUR

YSOBEL leaned against the bolted door and shook. Hot, nervous tears ran along her face and inside the neck of her cape, but she made no move to wipe them away. She was as aching and tired as if Evelake had indeed beaten her with his great, heavy hands, and she could not think. Gradually, and after a long time, her eyes began again to focus on the snug, safe house and take comfort from its warmth and security.

She unpinned her cape and hung it upon its accustomed peg and went to the fire. One of the villeins, probably old Anya, who had come with her mother from the west country, had lighted new rushes in all the little bowls and put away the pots Ysobel had made. Only this morning, she thought with a kind of wonder. It seemed a hundred moons ago. She sat on the bench and gradually the fire warmed her and the steady-burning lights drove the darkness a little from her heart and the aching and tiredness went away, leaving her quiet and empty.

She took a thin brass disk and struck it with a tiny hammer. After a moment Anya came, small and dark and unsmiling, as she had been since her mistress died. She stood, not speaking, waiting to know what Ysobel wanted, and Ysobel wondered what she *did* want beyond the sight of a familiar face and the sound of an ordinary, friendly voice. The dour Anya, she thought, was little help, and Ysobel suddenly would be rid of her again. "Bring me a bowl of barley broth, Anya," she said sharply, and remembered to add "please," though she did not feel for courtesy.

Anya said, "It is not enough, and you gone from this house without a bite at the noonstead eating."

"It is enough. Do as I say."

Anya pressed her lips together and went away glowering. She was back in a moment with a bowl, which she set beside the fire to warm and left again, silently and at once. When the fire released the sweet odors of the broth, rich with barley and meat juices, Ysobel lifted the bowl and drained it and put out the rushlights and laid aside her outer clothes and lay upon the rushes in her corner and covered herself with a wolfskin. She did not sleep. When Anya and the other villeins came to lie upon the floor, their feet to the fire for warmth, she kept her eyes closed in pretense.

Throughout the long night, she went over and over in her mind the scene with Evelake, hating the remembering but not able to stop it. She had always felt evil in him. Now she had seen it. Or thought she had seen it? Knowing Bran's love for him, and Carodoc's, she wondered even now if she were wrong. Could it be she who was full of malice or (she turned restlessly) bewitched to see evil where others saw only good?

She could not speak of these things—or thought she could not—to Carodoc. She must speak of them to someone. They had laid a burden upon her she did not want to carry alone.

Bran. Could she tell Bran all that had happened? She

imagined his unbelieving look, his laughter, even his anger, if she should tell him—and thought she could not. But she must. She must tell someone or lose her wits. She would have to risk Bran's displeasure. She would have to tell him, for there was no one else to tell. She *would* tell him, as soon as he should come. At once she felt more relaxed. She closed her eyes, wondering if sleep would come to her now.

She dreamed Bran was standing in the doorway. The sun streamed around him showing the house empty and swept. It was good to see him, even in a dream; good to let her dream-eyes rest upon his well-loved and crooked face. She wished she did not have to awaken and take up the burden of unhappiness that had been with her on her lying down. She was glad the sunlight could not reach her corner and wake her.

"Ysobel?"

His voice calling a question roused her to full waking. It was not a dream. He was here—her Bran—himself, not a shadow of her own wishing—in the doorway.

"Bran!" She shouted his name in her happiness and added more quietly, "It's late. Do you wait but a moment and I'll be with you."

"Hurry then, sleepyhead. It's not like you to be so late abed."

He went out into the cold, clear day and she threw aside the wolfskin and reached for her tunic in one swift motion. She pulled the dress over her head and put the torque about her shoulders helter-skelter, not bothering to adjust it properly, and snatched her cloak and went outside to join him.

He folded her in his arms and laid his cheek against her hair and the loneliness went away from her and the fear of loneliness. "Oh, but it's good to see you, Ysobel," he said as he released her. "I thought I would never get a day free from studying."

She laughed at him, seeing him rested and content, and took his hand, pulling him after her toward the lake. "Come with me while I wash the last of the sleep from my eyes."

They ran like young deer to the lake's edge and she scooped the icy water in her hands and dashed it against her face a time and a time again and felt her skin tingle and glow. When she had had enough, they went back to the house, and while he turned the fresh-killed duck, already sizzling above the fire, she shook out her braids and untangled them with a comb made from the antlers of a stag and plaited her hair again.

"Hurry, Ysobel," he called, peering into the shadowy corner. "It is ever like a woman to dally, and I am that hungry that I could eat the very roof pole."

"I'm coming. See. I am here."

He took the duck from the spit and divided it neatly and laid a half in each of their bowls. They thanked Beli for the grace of food and light and life and ate in silence until the duck was finished.

They talked of little things then. Of Bran's free day earned, he said, by hard study, which had put him a little ahead of his class of bards; of Carodoc's coming just as the moon was rising with word of the mistletoe and of the joy that word gave to Abiris; of themselves and their plans to wed now that Bran was a bard and would receive a bard's portion from the village storehouse.

As they talked, some of the happiness went out of Ysobel's face. The mistletoe and their hopes and plans brought back, sharp and clear, remembrance of the day just past, and she did not laugh and her eyes grew dark as the waters of the lake upon a stormy day.

Bran, watching her, wondered. It was not like Ysobel to be sad on the days when he could come to be with her. Perhaps, he thought, she would speak of what was troubling her if he ceased his own talk and gave her time and he waited, quiet, but she did not speak. He would not question her. He would not force her confidence, but he wished she would tell him.

She wanted to tell him, but fear of his ridicule was strong within her and kept her lips closed. The silence lengthened between them, uncomfortable, separating them, until it seemed to her to put on form and substance and fill the room. Bran got up and walked about the house, touching the cloth on her loom and the saddles hanging upon wall pegs and the studded bronze bowls that stood, for decoration, on the floor. She did not look at him.

When he could bear the silence no longer, he cried out to her, "What is it, Ysobel? What troubles your heart? Will you not tell me that I may help you? Do not shut out my love. Do not separate us who should be one in thought."

He sounded hurt and she thought I must tell him—I must —no matter what comes of it. I can not go on hurting him even if he laughs or is angry. She answered his pleading with a plea of her own. "You will not mock me, Bran? You will not say I am dreaming the thing I will tell you? You will not be angry?"

"You know I will not," he answered, and she held in a sigh, thinking she was not sure.

"It—it is Evelake."

She expected an outburst. She saw his face tighten and then saw him will himself to calm.

"Evelake. Yes. What has he done now?" In spite of his effort, he could not keep a little scorn from his voice, and she knew it was scorn for her.

She gulped and told him of the meeting yesterday and of what had come of it. Once started, she told it all—in a rush—lest she lose her courage before the gloom gathering in his face. When she had done, she sat, holding herself tight against whatever he might say.

For a long moment he did not say anything but looked into her face, not, she thought, seeing it. She wished, as she had so often wished before, that she could get past some barrier in him to the place he kept hidden even from her. She thought he did not know of the barrier or of the hidden place, did not shut her out purposely but because he could not help himself. He spoke finally, softly, and very slowly, as if he were thinking. "It is hard to know what to say, Ysobel. Evelake—Evelake *did* strike Carodoc, but I think—I am sure—he scarce knew what he was doing." He wished he could erase from his memory Evelake's accusations against himself. He would not speak of them to her, but they disturbed him all the more since she had spoken of her troubled heart. "I am sure he was sorry and did not have the courage to say so to Carodoc. For the rest, I think he was—was but teasing. Evelake is now and again gamesome of mind and sometimes he does not see the true effect of his games upon those he sports with."

She thought there had been no gamesomeness in Evelake last night. A part of her mind told her to leave it here, to accept Bran's explanation—or pretend to—and forget the whole thing. But she knew she would have no peace if she left it. She knew she must try again to make Bran see. "He was not teasing, Bran. You were not there. You did not see him or hear him. It—it was as if he were—were *bewitched.*"

He came to her and sat beside her and put his arm around her and spoke reasonably and gently. "Hear me, my sweeting. I have not seen Evelake since the night at Annwyn's hut, when he was—was not altogether his own man. But I know Evelake. And I *know*"—she wondered if there was a touch of defiance in his words—"there is no real evil in him. There is—there must be—some mistaking. Bewitched! Evelake is not one to let himself be set upon by witcheries. Maybe it is these whispers of witchcraft—yes, I have heard them, too —that give color to your thinking."

She shook her head. "Bran, no! You were not there. You did not see him or hear him."

"Hear me out, Ysobel. Evelake is—I say to you—in truth a—a good person. He is full of high spirits, sometimes wanton in his sportiveness, and sometimes unthinking. But not evil. He will explain his actions of last night. Let us find him and ask him about it and he will make all clear. Let us seek him now. Together."

She had no wish to see Evelake again. But maybe, she thought, Bran would see for himself some little of what she had seen, and that would be good. Only now—with a great opening of her mind—she realized that part of her own fear of Evelake was fear for Bran, fear that Evelake would, in some manner, out of ill humor and jealousy, do Bran a mischief. If Bran would only take warning, he could, in a measure, protect himself.

"Yes," she said, "let us go, Bran."

Evelake was not at his father's house. His mother, an overfat, simpering woman inclined to endless chatter, told them her good, kind boy had gone with a packet of food to poor, silly Annwyn, the Swineherd. She suggested they come in and wait for him and taste her honey cakes, which were surely the best in the village. Or perhaps Bran would like to see the brace of hunting hounds Ganhelon had but yesternight brought over from the mainland, where he kept his pack. They were fine hounds, though they needed a bit of training, and . . .

Bran got them away at last, courteously enough but firmly, leaving her looking after them, still talking.

"Isn't she a very hellhound?" Ysobel asked, laughing. Bran laughed, too, and agreed, and they were both glad of the incident and of the silly, vain woman, for she had served to break down the wall they had built between them.

"What now?" Ysobel asked.

"It's a fine day." There was still an edge of laughter in Bran's voice. He looked at the bright November sky. "Too fine. The weather will break soon and then we'll likely not see sun for many days. Let us go to meet Evelake on his return from Annwyn's."

She had half hoped Evelake's absence from home would put an end to Bran's plan to talk to him. She should, she thought wryly, have known better. Her Bran was not easily turned from any purpose. Besides, there was still the unmasking of Evelake. She nodded agreement and they crossed the lake and made the dugout fast on the other bank. Bran straightened from knotting the thong and looked at the great, dark Tor stark against the bright sky and shivered.

"What is it, Bran?" Ysobel asked quickly and he answered, "I do not like the Tor. It—it seems to me a dark and fearful place—a place, maybe, of doom. I wish—I wish we had not climbed it."

"What ails you, Bran?" She was amazed at him. She had not thought there was so much superstition in him. He sounded as mystically frightened as Carodoc, but with none of Carodoc's excuse of the blood of ancient people. "You did not feel so when we stood at the top and watched our friend grow smaller and smaller among the swamps and forests."

"*Your* friend, not mine," he said quickly.

"But, Bran," she began, and stopped, having no words to go on.

"Joshua ben Joseph." His voice sounded bemused, a little bitter. "I do not understand him and his everlasting talk of kindness and mercy—or his god, who is so strange, wanting no sacrifice but some—some vague kind of goodness. I do not understand him and I fear him and his teaching."

"*Fear* him, Bran! You are but teasing. How could you fear so gentle and peaceable——"

He stopped her with an impatient gesture of his hand. "I do not fear the *man*, Ysobel. You were not listening. It is his thinking, his *words* that bring fear to my mind. I fear the witchery of his words. I tell you he put upon me a spell so strong that there are times—there are times when I even question the teachings of the *Druids!*"

The last words were spoken so softly she scarcely heard them, and they brought a rush of guilt to her as she remembered her own traitor thoughts about the stranger's god. Because of that memory, she spoke sharply. "Don't say such things, Bran. Joshua ben Joseph was no spell-flinging warlock but a simple, good man. And what is there to doubt in the worship of light-giving Beli?"

He turned to her quickly, almost angrily. "The burnings, for one thing. It is not—it *cannot* be good and right to kill people so—even wrongdoers, even witches and warlocks and murderers, in sacrifice to the god. Yet the Druids say Beli wills it. I would never have doubted their words if I had not listened to Joshua ben Joseph, and it is not good that a bard should doubt the teachings."

She nodded slowly. "Yes. I have thought such things, too. But it is an ancient custom. The Druids are wise and good. It may be right and needful and the will of Beli. And it

59

may be a time will come when there will be no more burnings because there will be no more wrongdoings or witchings."

He scowled at her. "Have you lost your wits? There will always be wrongdoers and witches and dark deeds upon the night. And there will always be the burnings. Besides, there are other troubling things I would not have seen before—before *he* came."

"What things?" She thought he was opening his secret door—at least a crack—and she wasn't sure she liked it. She found his doubts frightening and she felt unable to help him and miserable.

"Oh—things." He paused and went on unwillingly, as if he had to say what he did not wish to put into words. "I tell you, Ysobel, our priests are not—not all good and wise. You well know they hold much power, hold it in trust for Beli to use for the good of his people. But some of them—some of them do not so. Some use their power in wrong ways, not for the people, but to better their own lot. There are—I fear it—more do so than you would think. Too many more. Not Abiris. He stands by the old, true ways. He is upright and strong. But he is blind to the others. He does not or will not see the rottenness. But it is there, Ysobel. I feel it. I know it. Yet I cannot prove it. But it *is* there, and it is creeping, creeping." He turned abruptly away from her and started toward the forest path.

She stood where she was, feeling cold along her backbone. What was happening to her and to Bran? In the late watches of how many nights had she lain upon her bed and fought the questions that came unasked into her mind? It was not only the burnings, though they were evil enough. There were other things, things she could not truly put a name to but that seemed, nonetheless, terrible. Was it right for the priests to have such power that even the rulers of the tribes were subject to them? Was it right that none could study except by their good will? Was it right that they and only they should have the power of life and death over all the people? There was an evil something creeping about them all like a miasma from the lake, as Bran had said, and she feared it as she feared the dark mysteries in the Druid's lore that were beginning to escape the bonds put upon them by the old, wise, just laws and become instruments of personal power. She had told herself that her fears were groundless, the imaginings of a restless mind working in secret in the night. But now she knew Bran had the same fears and the same doubts and she felt suddenly lost.

Suppose they *were* right, she and Bran? Suppose the Druids were no longer true guardians of Beli's will? Suppose —suppose Beli himself . . .

She dared not finish that thought. She ran after Bran, quoting to his back the articles of their belief, as if there were in them a magic to dispel such thoughts.

> *In every person there is a soul:*
> *In every soul there is an intelligence;*
> *In every intelligence there is thought;*
> *In every thought there is good or evil;*
> *In every evil there is death;*
> *In every good there is life:*
> *In every life there is god.*
> *Death is but the mid-point of life.*

She thought he checked a little in his stride, listening, and she said belligerently, because she was herself no longer sure, "Can these things breed evil, Bran? Can justice and law and good government and the grace of wisdom breed evil? I do not believe it!"

Bran did not want to answer her. He was angry with himself that he had been lured into talk of Joshua ben Joseph. Why had she mentioned that kind, just man who had started him thinking along lines that ran against his faith? He, Bran the Brave, had almost managed to argue away his doubts of the Druids, and now it was all to do over. Why could he not be let to forget Joshua ben Joseph and his talk of a stranger god of love and mercy?

He did not slow his steps to wait for her but he spoke over his shoulder, harsh words to cover his own distress of mind. "You, Ysobel, you are—are but a child in your thinking. You see only what you want to see. Let us talk of it no more. I should have kept silence."

She was rebuffed and knew it and the knowledge hurt her and she said no more until they saw Annwyn's hut ahead of them. He stopped walking then and put his arms around her and kissed the top of her head and said, "I am sorry, birdling. I shouldn't trouble you with my dark thinking. You are right, of course, and I'll send these groping doubts away and think no more about them. Come, let us see if Evelake is within yonder."

She started to speak her own doubts to him but feared to rouse him again and did not. They went on toward the hut, hand in hand. His kindness had healed her hurt somewhat, but she knew in her heart he still thought of her as a child and she knew she had somehow failed him when he needed her.

A strange, gobbling sound, a sound as if someone were hurt or afraid, came to them. Bran stopped and dropped her hand and set his head on one side, listening. The sound came again and seemed to come from within Annwyn's hut.

"Come!" Bran said, and began to run the last few feet to the door. "Evelake's in some trouble!"

She ran behind him and was but a step away when he thrust at the door and it swung inward, letting in the sun. They saw Annwyn crouched in a corner, his eyes upon Evelake, who was hammering the sharpened end of a bronze pin into his own leg.

Evelake was so bent upon what he was doing he had not heard their coming. "Kneel, dog," he said to Annwyn; "kneel and bow your head before your lord and master."

Ysobel whispered, "What——" and Bran put his hand over her mouth to hush her. Annwyn, moaning and gobbling, fell upon his knees and tried to speak. His eyes were wide and dull and his face was drained of color, drawn up in fear. He opened his mouth, but no words came. And Evelake said, "Speak up, Swineherd; name me your lord."

Annwyn gulped and managed to stammer, his voice shaking, "Yea, L-l-lord. You—you d-do be m-m-my master. You do be L-l-lord of D-d-d-darkness and I y-y-your faithful servant in all things." He fell upon his face and his body writhed like a snake.

Evelake said inexorably, "And you will be my slave forever and do my bidding no matter what it may be."

Annwyn tried to move and could not and Bran hurled himself into the room, yelling, "Enough, Evelake. Enough of this terrifying. Leave the poor witless creature alone."

Evelake looked at Bran and at Ysobel, who was just behind him, and smiled as if he had been having no more than a quiet, friendly talk with Annwyn. He removed the pin from his leg and got up. Ysobel could see a droplet of blood where the pin had been. "Beli bless you, Bran and Ysobel. What do you here?"

Annwyn, released from Evelake's eyes, had stumbled to

his feet and was sidling to the door, watching Evelake with fear and horror upon his face. Ysobel put out a hand to stop him. She wanted to comfort and reassure him, to wipe away the fear with kindliness, but he evaded her and slid out into the day and, at once, she heard the thud of his feet as if he ran for his life.

Evelake said, "Welcome, Bran, my friend. I——" but Bran would not let him finish and Ysobel had never seen Bran so angry. His voice came tight and controlled.

"You—filthy—swine, using that old *trick* to frighten the poor silly creature. You know it's but a—a means the Druids use in their teaching to show us the workings of the body. Anyone can do it. Anyone."

Ysobel found relief in the words though she did not fully understand their meaning. As she had watched Evelake, she had felt in her own mind an echo of Annwyn's terror and superstitious awe even while her good sense told her there must be a reasonable explanation. Later, when they were away from this place, she would ask Bran how this thing could be.

"You know," Bran was saying. "You well know, Evelake, we are forbidden to show the unlearned these things unless we are ourselves endangered and have real need to frighten. No one in all the teaching groves—no true man of the Druids—would use such a shift to frighten a poor fool out of his remaining wits."

He stopped to draw breath and Evelake said softly, "I am no Druid, Bran, nor ever will be. Remember?"

Bran thundered at him. "But you took the oath and you are bound by it to the end of time. You should be shamed, Evelake, as I am shamed for you, that you so far forget your own—your own honor and your duty as a free man and

64

play upon the dark mind of such a one as Annwyn. Lord of Darkness indeed! I—I should *thrash* you, Evelake."

Evelake's face was red and his eyes held a gleam of danger, but he said quietly—too quietly, Ysobel thought, "Try it, Bran. Just try it!" His fists, she saw, and shivered seeing it, were tight balls and the muscles of his arms were huge and taut.

Bran did not move.

"Are you afraid then, Bran? Bran the Brave?" Evelake taunted him and Bran answered, *"Afraid?* Of you? That I am not. You know it is forbidden a bard to strike any man in anger."

"Words," Evelake said. "No one here will go tattling to your masters. I will not, I promise you, and Ysobel is not likely to carry tales about her own true love." The last words were sneered and Ysobel wanted to protest, but he gave her no chance. "You have belittled me with your talk, Bran. It is my right to prove upon your body who is the better man."

Bran did not move or speak.

"Then you are a coward, Bran. As I thought."

Bran looked at him and Ysobel thought she'd never seen such contempt in any look and she was glad, for now she was sure Bran knew in truth the kind of man Evelake was.

"Coward! Coward! Coward!" Evelake's voice rose in hysteria and Ysobel called sharply, "Look *out*, Bran," but knew she had called in vain. Bran stood quietly while Evelake struck him with such force he fell to the floor, and the whole hut shuddered with the force of his fall.

Evelake started toward him, raging still, and Ysobel stepped between them, seeing Bran, for the moment, stunned by his fall. "Will you strike me, too, for a coward, Evelake?"

she said, and wondered at her even calm, for she was not sure he would not strike her.

Evelake checked himself, although she thought it took a great effort, and looked at her as if he were surprised to see her and turned away.

Bran got up, rubbing his jaw. He spoke to Evelake's back and each word had in it the sound of an icicle breaking after a night of black frost. "If ever I see you at such tricks again, Evelake, or hear of it, I shall have you brought before the Druids under charge of intimidating a member of the tribe. You are—you must be still sick with your failure to pass the tests. If I did not think so, I should not wait to accuse you."

Evelake did not look at Bran for a long moment. Ysobel saw his shoulders shake but whether with anger or his twisted laughter she could not judge. When he turned to them, his face was almost merry and he smiled at Bran and came and put his arm about Bran's stiff shoulders and squeezed them affectionately and said, "Forgive me, Bran, for being so angered by your talk. You know me well. You know how quickly temper rises in me. I thought you unkind and unfair and I—I lost my head. I would not hurt you, my friend, my old, sworn friend."

Ysobel, watching, saw Bran's face soften and the icy look leave his eyes. He believes him, she thought. The great, simple fool *believes* Evelake.

Evelake went on. "As for the trick with the pin, Bran, I was but having a little sport with Annwyn. By the five sacred symbols at the door, I swear it. I meant no harm. You cannot think the jest was ill-meant. I'll set all right with Annwyn and I'll have a care not to jest so again. He is so easy to fool he tempts me past bearing. But I'll guard my

66

sportiveness, Bran. Forgive me and put the whole thing from your mind."

Bran's face was almost comical in its look of relief and Ysobel despaired of making him see the truth. One day—she was sure of it—Evelake would do him a real injury, but, likely, Bran would go on trusting his "friend" even if Evelake stuck a knife in his heart. Bran the Brave! He should be called rather Bran the Foolish. He was, in himself, too wholesome of nature to believe ill of anyone for long. Well, *she* would not trust Evelake. No matter how he simpered and crawled and apologized. No matter what promises he gave or oaths he swore. Had she not his own word for it that promises are made to be broken! And, likely, oaths were the same to him.

Bran was speaking—speaking joyously and generously. "I should have known, Evelake. I should have known. It is rather I should be begging your forgiveness for lack of trust. Come, let us go home together and tomorrow we will find Annwyn and calm his fear."

He did not look at Ysobel. He had, she thought, for the moment, forgotten she was there, and she was glad of a space in which to compose her face to blankness. She had no wish now for Bran to know her heart, for in his new-found belief in Evelake he would not easily endure her skeptical mind. She saw Evelake watching her and she thought, he knows I do not believe him but it does not matter. He knows, too, I cannot make Bran see the truth, and it is only Bran he wants to befuddle with his easy talk.

Evelake said, "No, Bran. Do you take Ysobel back to the village. I will wait here for the poor swineherd that he may not have to spend a night in fear of me. We will talk again, Bran, my friend, before you go back to Abiris. I shall not be long in coming after you."

67

Bran said, "So be it, for it is likely better so." He turned and saw Ysobel behind him and looked guilty, knowing he had forgotten her and put his arm through hers and said, "Come, birdling, let us go home."

"Bran," she asked, as soon as they were away from the hut, "how could Evelake do to himself what we saw and feel no pain?"

Bran considered a moment, frowning. "These things are mysteries of the priests, Ysobel," he said, "and of right you should not know of them. But you have seen and you'd best understand. You know that there is much about the mind and the body of man that is known to the Druids and not to ordinary folk. This is part of the secret lore that has been passed from Druid to Druid in the teaching groves since a time so ancient it is lost to the memory of man. One of the secrets is this: there are places upon the body free of pain—small numb patches in the skin. If you know where they are and if you know how to tighten the sinews about them and just how to hammer home the pin, you can do what Evelake did without feeling hurt."

"Oh," she said. "So simple a thing. But it has the look of magic when you do not know how it is done."

"Yes," Bran said. "And Evelake was wrong to frighten the poor swineherd. But he will not do so again."

She wanted to deny his belief, but she would not. They went quickly to the lake and home. It was not until next day that she remembered they had said nothing to Evelake about his meeting with her. Just as well, she thought. He'd have explained *that*, too, to my trusting Bran.

CHAPTER FIVE

THE ground was covered with snow as Ysobel walked between her father and Carodoc along the forest path to cut the mistletoe. Heavy gray clouds pressed close upon the frozen earth on this sixth day of the new moon. Soon would come the long dark night when Beli hid his light for more than fifteen hours by the water clock.

She remembered that Joshua ben Joseph had told her he had been born at this time of the year upon a night when the stars shone with extra fire as they did in winter. There had been a special great star that had moved across the heavens and some men had said it was a portent. She wondered how he was faring with the thing he had to do and remembered the sadness that came, at times, upon him and hoped he was well. She wished she could see him again, for, in spite of the mistletoe waiting to be cut, she was troubled, and he had had a wonderful power to charm away trouble and bring comfort in its stead.

Abiris said, "We are nearly there. Beli was generous and the bough is large and heavy with berries. There is enough to cure all sickness and bring fertility to our women and our cattle and our crops."

Ysobel took a little skipping step, as she used to do when

69

she was a child. This was no time for troubled thoughts. This was the best of all the many ceremonies of the year. It was, too, specially good that the blessing had been sent to their own grove. It was an honor to Abiris, a sign that Beli looked with favor upon his priest. And well he might, she thought, for Abiris was taller and finer and better and wiser than any other Druid. His gold-brown hair, just touched with gray, fell abundantly about his shoulders. He carried the Druid's ash staff as if it were a banner, not a crutch to lean upon, and his finespun robe was whiter than the untrodden snow at the edge of the path.

On her other side, Carodoc carried a white cloth and led the white bullock. Ahead of them they could see the people of the village waiting. Everyone was there, even the babies, even the old and the sick, wrapped in furs, lovingly carried upon hides stretched between poles or in the arms of their younger and stronger friends.

The people opened a path for them and Abiris walked along it, erect and solemn, as befitted a priest. Carodoc led the white ox away, and Ysobel took her stand in the front rank of the crowd, as was her right. She looked about her for Bran and smiled at her own foolishness, knowing he would be waiting somewhere out of sight. At a little distance from her she saw Evelake and, with him, Annwyn, still with fear in his eyes. She thought Evelake had not explained the pin trick, for, if he had, Annwyn would not still be fear-haunted. She was not surprised. She had not expected Evelake to take away his fear. He was, she was sure, intent to bind Annwyn to his will for some evil purpose and was using fear as his cudgel. She tried to catch Evelake's eyes, to let him know she understood what he was doing, but he did not see her or—which was more probable—was avoiding her deliberately.

70

Carodoc tied the ox to a young beech that companioned the mistletoe oak and came to stand beside her. He signed to Evelake to join them but, again, Evelake did not or would not see.

Abiris raised his arms above his head and the chattering crowd hushed and the grove was still. He intoned a prayer of thanks to Beli. The deep, half-sung notes vibrated through the crowd.

He finished the prayer and Bran came forward from the shadow of a tree and laid his hand upon the thong of the ox, ready to unloose it. From somewhere behind her someone hissed and someone else spoke softly a single word.

"Warlock."

Ysobel thought she had imagined the sound, but another whispered the dread word and she realized, with a shock, the accusation was directed at Bran. She looked about her, trying to see the whisperers, but she could not tell who had spoken. She wondered whether she should call out to Abiris. He had not heard, she was sure, for he was going calmly about his priestly duties. But it would not do to offend the god when the sacrifice was being prepared and, besides, the crowd was silent now. She looked about her again and saw the crooked Annwyn begin to pass quickly and secretly to and fro among the people, and where he passed the whispers began again. She guessed Annwyn was spreading this poison. At Evelake's bidding? She was ready enough to believe it, but she could not say for sure, and it mattered little. Annwyn must be stopped. Beside her stood Carodoc, his ears and mind were closed to everything except the ceremony at the oak, and she knew he'd not hear her if she spoke quietly to him. She'd go after Annwyn herself and charge him with spreading lies and stop him. She shifted her position preparatory to edging through the people behind her with the least fuss and heard the crowd's gasp. She looked toward Abiris and saw his arm with the knife of sacrifice raised to kill the beast and knew she must not profane the god by any movement.

The ox was killed and the Thanksgiving sacrifice offered to Beli. Abiris moved in the following stillness until he was beneath the bough that held the mistletoe and carefully kirtled his long robe and began to climb the oak, a golden sickle in the belt of his robe.

Above the grove the drifting scud of cloud broke and pale sunlight touched the sickle and it flashed bright and shimmering. The crowd cheered. Beli had blessed the ceremony with his own light. It was a good omen. Abiris swung the sickle and, with one stroke, cut the mistletoe and let it fall into a white cloth below and descended from the tree. He lifted the branch from the cloth and held it high so that all could see. The sun was hidden again by the wrack, but no one minded. The bough was large and richly covered with the white waxy berries the villeins called All Heal. This would be a good year with food enough for all. The people were content.

They went quickly from the grove, anxious to get out of the cold that clawed at spines and reddened noses. Two boys brought the cloth, folded neatly, to Carodoc. Abiris joined his son and daughter, smiling at them.

Ysobel wondered as they walked back through the forest whether she should tell Abiris what she had heard. She decided she should do so for her own peace of mind and Bran's safety. The whisperings should be stopped at once, before they grew more serious, but she knew it was almost impossible to stop whispers when you could not name the whisperers. Perhaps her father, in his wisdom, would have a plan.

When they were in the house and had driven the cold from their bones with mead and the roasted pig the villeins had left crackling on the fire, she told Abiris all she had heard and seen at the cutting of the mistletoe. He listened carefully. He was, she thought, startled at first, and frowned, but when she had come to the end of her tale his face showed smooth again and untroubled.

"Cease your fearing, my daughter," he said. "There are always murmurings among the villeins, now of one evil thing, now of another, for landless men are ever like to be discontented and these murmurs are but the outward signs of their restlessness. Words are fruitless things when there is no substance of evil or good behind them, and have in themselves no power to harm. No witchings have been named to the Druids. This is but superstitious chatter that comes with the long nights when there is too little to occupy empty heads and the memories of old beliefs are in the air. It will die for lack of substance to feed upon."

"But Bran, father. I am sure the whispers were meant for him and I fear for him. The very charge of witchcraft in those empty heads you speak of could breed real danger for him."

"I doubt it, Ysobel. It may well be that there is"—he looked at Carodoc's face, half hidden in shadows, and Ysobel wondered if he were thinking of Evelake—"someone who does not like our Bran, who is perhaps jealous of him. But no one suffers for witchcraft because of words, my daughter. There must be witness of creatures—or people—or crops bewitched before the judges will condemn, and there's been no shadow of such witness these many moons. Indeed," he smiled, "Beli would lack for sacrifice at the great circle if the whole of the land were as law-abiding as our people."

73

Ysobel said, "How *can* the judges be sure?" and her father answered calmly, "There are tests, Ysobel. Tests handed down from generation to generation, and they do not fail. There are, too, signs only the Druids know. Neither Bran nor any other will be burned in the wicker cage without true cause. Think no more of such things."

She remembered Bran's charge that too many Druids were forgetting their duty and the holiness of their office and she wondered if there were, among them, any who might see signs that were not there for the sake of silver coins Evelake could offer them. She was sure Evelake was the jealous one her father had mentioned. She wanted to cry out her suspicions but she did not. She would not hurt her brother in his love of Evelake. Besides, no matter how lost to Beli other Druids might be, her father was strict and upright in his dealings and he would want proof of any accusation she might bring. She had no proof—only Bran's fear and her own that the old, proud company was no longer all selfless to serve the god and the people, and her suspicions against Evelake. She hid her face so it would not show her continuing trouble and her father and Carodoc spoke quietly of other things, forgetting her, until it was time for Abiris to go back to his teaching.

But he had not entirely forgotten her troubled heart nor been misled by her hidden face. As he lifted the door latch he spoke again of the accusation of witchcraft. "Do not worry, Ysobel. There is no need," and when she could not give him a lighthearted answer he added, "Tomorrow I will send Bran to you. Tell him what you have told me. He may convince you that there is nothing to fear and, if he cannot, a woman's mind being a set and stubborn thing, you will at least know he is warned."

74

"Yes," she agreed. "I can, at least, warn him. Thank you, my father." But she wondered whether Bran would believe any warning, and without his belief nothing would profit her telling him.

He came early next day, swinging along the cobbled lanes, his face bright with cold and good health. Expecting him, Ysobel had given the villeins tasks away from the house so there would be no one to overhear their talk.

She told him at once all the tale of the whisperings, forcing her mind and her voice to a steady, dispassionate recital of the facts, accusing no one. He listened gravely, not interrupting, but she could see no sign of strain or worry caused by the tale.

When she had finished, he reassured her much as Abiris had done, careful not to belittle her fears. "Look you, birdling. These are nothing but the vaporings of people who must have something for the amusement of their minds. They turn their thoughts inward at the times of hard frost and think upon the ancient beliefs of their forefathers. It does not matter to them, for they are only venting their need to make a little excitement in the endless procession of dull days the cold time brings to them. As for me—I was there beside the mistletoe tree, suddenly, where I had not been before, as if I had indeed appeared by magic, and they made their whispers and forgot them in the larger, grander excitement of the sacrifice and the cutting of the sacred bough. You heard nothing when the crowd broke up to return to their houses, because they had already forgotten. Besides, my girl, how much have I been in the village these three moons past? Have you ever heard of a warlock who can cast his spells from three leagues off? Cease your fretting, my sweet, and let me see the laughter again in your eyes."

75

There was, she thought, something in what he said, though she'd not put it past Evelake to get around his absence. If, indeed, this *were* a plot of Evelake's and not a monster of her own creating. At any rate, Bran had been warned, as clearly as she knew how to warn him. She had done what she could and she forced the remaining unease out of her mind. There was no sense in spoiling this day. She saw him seldom enough and never for long. She'd best make the most of it now. She looked at him and managed to laugh a little.

"That is better," he said, and kissed her. "Now listen, for there is a thing I've been near bursting to tell you."

"Good?" she asked, beginning to sparkle to the sparkling of his mood.

"Good," he said, and waited, teasing her.

"Well. Go *on*, my good lump of swine fat. Do not keep me forever hanging on the wind of your words."

"Guess."

She stamped her foot on the earth floor. "I'll *not* guess, Bran. How *can* I guess? Do you tell me quickly or I'll— I'll do something dreadful to you."

He grinned at her, delighted that she had risen to his teasing. "Peace, peace," he said. "Don't afright me with your threats!" He lifted an arm as if he would protect himself from her. "I'll tell you."

His look was suddenly proud and pleased and a little solemn and she thought whatever his news was it touched him nearly. When he spoke, the sound of his voice was the sound of awe and humility. "The Arch Druid has sent for me, Ysobel. He is sending his own bard upon a journey to Brittany to learn new songs. The Arch Druid has heard of my singing and harping. He wants me to come

76

to Carleon—to stay there for a time and a time and sing for him when he would rest his mind."

She put her arms about him and held him joyfully. "Oh, Bran, Bran, Bran. This is the greatest honor that could come to any bard. And you but newly dressed in the blue robe. You'll go all the way to Carleon beyond our forests and the estuary to the very edge of Cymru itself and see the Arch Druid. See him and talk to him and sit at his board. And . . . oh, *Bran!*"

She muffled her head against his shoulder, realizing that he would be many leagues away and she would not see him for long and dreary nights. She did not want to spoil his pleasure by one whit, but he sensed her trouble and in a measure shared it. "I doubt I shall be long away, Ysobel. No more than the waxing and the waning of a single moon, perhaps, and I shall miss you—every hour I shall miss you and I shall carry you in my heart the whole time of absence."

She lifted her face and there was no sign of trouble in it now. "Of course, Bran," she said, "and I shall send my thoughts flying straight to you as the falcon flies at the sun; only my thoughts will need no unleashing, being free to go to you at will. When you come home again you'll tell me of all the wonders at Carleon and what you saw upon the way. When—when do you leave, Bran?"

"In a week. A month. I know not. When the Arch Druid sends his word. I shall set out from here, Ysobel, and so see you again before I go." He turned quickly away from her, conscious of the heaviness of his own heart at the thought of being so far from her. He had not, in truth, thought of it before, being filled with pride and joy at the summons. He knew she was hard put to it not to weep at the prospect of loneliness and he picked up the bundle he had brought with him and gave it to her. "Look, Ysobel. I brought my other robe. A little hole has found its way—though by what means I know not—into the cloth at the back. Will you mend it for me?"

She undid the bundle, grateful for his care to set their two minds for a moment upon other matters, and laughed aloud to see that the little hole was indeed a great rent. He must have walked straight through a bramblebush, she thought.

"You'd better leave it, Bran. Your little hole will take a deal of mending. I'll send it on to you by one of the villeins when it is done. What a great oaf you are, going about with your eyes upon the heavens and your mind Beli alone knows where." She smiled and let her love shine through to him that he would not mind her scolding.

He looked at her as if he'd been a small boy caught in a great mischief. "Don't scold, Ysobel." His words had a solemn sound, but his face told her he knew she was not truly vexed. "I was thinking as I walked and I did not see the bramble. Truly. Besides, I knew you'd not mind the mending, for your hands are clever and your heart is kind. I'll leave the robe with you. Fix the rent in your own good time, but come with me now. I would borrow Carodoc's great bow and his flights of arrows. I've had little time of late to train my eye and the muscles in my arm and they are getting dull and weak. Abiris has been scolding me for not keeping my body at top fitness as the laws demand of us."

She thought his eye would never be dull and she could see for herself that the great muscles in his arm were as tight and taut as the bowstring they would pull. But she knew how he loved to split a willow wand or bring down a duck in flight and she was glad to go wherever he wanted so long as they two were together.

78

CHAPTER SIX

Bran came into the anteroom of the Arch Druid's chamber expecting his new friend, Peredur, to be there before him. Tomorrow, before the sun rose, he would be on his way home and he would be glad. He had been twenty-eight nights in the service of the Arch Druid and they had been a good time, full of new sights and sounds and thoughts. He had even lost most of his plaguing doubts about the priesthood to which he aspired, in the presence of the old man, who seemed so noble and wise and who was the chief priest of them all. But he was glad to be going home.

Peredur was not waiting for him. The guard at the door of the treasury, a taciturn young man with a long scar on his face, did not know where the captain might be. Bran sat before the fire and, half dozing with its warmth, remembered his setting out for Carleon on the first day of the new moon in the second month of winter.

The whole village, his village in the lake, had come to set him on his journey, proud that one of theirs had been honored by the Arch Druid. They had come—all of them— to the landing, and there had been none among them, he was sure, but wished him well. In spite of his assurances to Ysobel, the accusations of witchcraft at the cutting of the mistletoe had distressed and worried him. No man would feel happy at being branded a warlock. So he had watched and listened closely at his setting out for a renewal of the whispers. There had been none. There had been nothing but cries of "Beli speed you, Bran the Bard," and "Come home to us safe and soon, Bran," and small gifts for the journey. Best of all, there had been Evelake. The old, familiar, loved Evelake, smiling and clapping his shoulder and wishing him a happy stay in the great town. There had been no sign in Evelake of the wildness and cruelty and quick shifts of mood that had beset him of late. There had been no sign that Evelake held Bran in less than the old, close friendship of all the years of their growing up.

It was a pity Evelake was not here now, waiting with him for Peredur. He should have been. Until yesterday Evelake, with his shadow, Annwyn, had been in Carleon. Bran smiled, thinking of his own surprise when he had come upon Evelake at the leatherworker's. He had come, Evelake said, to see how Bran was faring, not knowing he would so soon be home again. They had spent many hours together in the days that followed while the Arch Druid was busy about his work, needing no harping or singing. Bran had told Evelake about his stay and about Peredur, captain of the Arch Druid's guard, and Evelake had promised to come tonight, when Peredur himself would guard the Arch Druid's treasure for the late watch. Then, Bran had said, they would go together, he and Evelake, home to their own people.

But yesterday a messenger had come from Evelake. Ganhelon had sent a man riding hard to bid his son away. His father needed Evelake, the rider had explained, to go quickly to the shore of the great sea, where even now ten brace of fine hunting hounds waited to be delivered to Brittany. Their handler had taken suddenly sick of a fever and was not able to go with them. Evelake was leaving at once, taking time only to provide food for his travels and to send word to his friend, Bran the Brave.

Well, it couldn't be helped, Bran thought, though he was disappointed. Evelake was ever a good son. He would lose no time in carrying out Ganhelon's request, and Bran honored him for it. Still, the long leagues would seem longer without a friend upon the path and he had looked forward to more good talk with Evelake. He saw too little of his friend since they no longer studied together in the teaching grove. Perhaps it was best after all that Evelake had failed his tests. The disciplines of the priesthood were hard and Evelake did not take kindly to discipline. There had been that time in Annwyn's hut. Bran found himself still troubled by the memory of the cowering swineherd. But surely Evelake had put that right, else Annwyn would not be so willingly his companion.

Where *was* Peredur? He'd promised to show Bran the Arch Druid's jewel, the great chevron bead encased in gold, which the people called the egg and was the symbol of the Arch Druid's power and the badge of his office. The jewel, sacred to Beli, was kept in the treasury under guard, for it had special properties and had been blessed of Beli himself in the ancient times. Bran wondered why he wanted so much to see the bead at close hand. He had seen it often enough at the great festivals when the Arch Druid wore it about his neck. He thought it was because the bead was so holy a symbol. If he could but touch it, he would himself be blessed.

The door of the anteroom was thrown open and Peredur strode into the place. Bran watched his new friend with affection. Peredur never just walked. He moved like an army after victory, full of vibrant life and laughter and good fellowship. He tossed his oxhide shield in a corner and stood his tall spear beside it and unbuckled his sword and laid it aside and loosened his leather breastplate.

"Forgive me that I was long in coming, Bran," he said. "Someone thought he had seen a stranger skulking near the Druid's house and raised an alarm and I must turn out the guard and search the whole of Carleon."

"Did you find anything of danger?"

"A mongrel dog and nothing more. The whole place is jumpy since word came that the Belgae are marauding some fifty leagues to the east. Fifty leagues! You'd think they were in Carleon itself."

He sat before the fire and stretched his long legs to the flame. "I'm wet through," he grumbled, "and tired as a hound. How I hate the rains, even if they do bring good growth from the corn. Are you full ready for your journey, friend Bran?"

"Yes." Bran smiled, thinking how little time he had needed for his preparations. The Arch Druid had ordered food to last him the three-day's journey home. He would pick up the packet tomorrow morning on his setting out. His extra robe, beautifully mended by Ysobel, and his shoes were neatly rolled and ready, waiting, and his harp he had with him. Those were his only belongings.

"Then do you sing to me a little while I rest my bones before I show you that which I promised."

Bran took his harp and sang a war song and a song of love and another that told of the coming of the ancestors. While he sang he looked a last time about the room. It was a bare place and, except near the fire, shadowy—a guardroom, nothing more. The scar-faced guard stood straight and silent as a tree beside the locked door of the treasury. A flagon of mead and two drinking horns were ready on a bench near the outer door. Peredur's horn was bordered with silver and a silver stag's head wreathed in ivy leaves was embossed upon one side. Peredur was proud of his horn. It had belonged to his father, a gift from a chieftain in recognition of long and true service. Peredur used it only upon special occasions and Bran was pleased that he had ordered it set out for their leave-taking. Even in the shadows the silver gleamed. Peredur must have taken care that one of the villeins should polish it and make it bright and beautiful for their parting pledge. The other horn was plain, but it would do as well for holding mead when the time came.

Peredur had been listening with his eyes closed. He straightened as the song-story ended. "Thank you, my friend," he said; "your harping and singing have much refreshed me." He laughed, deep and full. "There'll be few poor soldiers this night can boast of entertainment by the Arch Druid's harper."

Bran said, "Arch Druid's harper no longer, Peredur. Tonight and hereafter for many moons only Bran the Bard, learner under Abiris."

"But not for always, Bran." Peredur spoke with intent seriousness. "In ten years you'll be a Druid and someday, I'll warrant, you yourself will wear the Arch Druid's chevron jewel and I'll be telling proudly of the time you played me to rest."

Bran said simply, meaning each word, "You spin a cobweb dream, Peredur. I am the least of the bards. There are many and many more worthy than I."

Peredur made a gesture of disbelief. "We shall see who's spinning cobwebs, Bran. Come, let me show you the egg as I promised. Maybe it will bring you luck to touch it."

He took a rushlight and lit it at the fire and they went to the door of the treasury. Peredur spoke to the guard and received the key from him and unlocked the little door. He held the rushlight high and motioned Bran within and came after him while the guard watched. The treasury was little more than a cupboard. Outlines of chests showed dimly in the shadows. The Arch Druid's ceremonial robe of fine white wool hung stretched upon two pegs. A heavy gold pin winked on the shoulder and three rays were embroidered in gold upon the cloth. Near it, on a stone shelf, was the egg, a clear, glass bead surrounded by a sunburst of gold. The Arch Druid's chevron bead, sacred to Beli. Bran reached out his hand and touched it lightly, briefly, feeling full of awe, as if he were in the very presence of the god. He was still for a time, saying within himself a prayer for the health and safety of the Arch Druid and thanks for the honor shown him; then he backed out of the little door. Peredur came after him and waited while the guard formally checked the egg and the robe, the golden pin and torque, and the chests that held, Bran knew, the Arch Druid's store of silver coins. When he was satisfied, the scar-faced man relocked the door and gave Peredur the key. He was a little bored and a little amused by Bran's enchantment, but it did not matter.

"Well, Bran"—Peredur was smiling—"you have seen the egg and touched it. I hope you were not disappointed."

"No," Bran said, and could say no more for the awe that was still with him.

"Then," Peredur said, "we'd best make our farewells."

He went to the bench by the door and poured the mead into the two horns, brought them to the fire, and handed the plain one to Bran. The two men drained them. Peredur said, "May you come safe home, Bran the Bard, and may you come soon again to Carleon, my friend."

84

Bran thanked him and turned to get his harp and his cloak and back again for a final farewell. Peredur was swaying a little, as if he were suddenly ill.

Bran caught his arm. "What is it, Peredur?" he asked. "You are not well. Let me arouse one of the other men to stand your guard tonight."

Peredur passed his hand over his eyes and smiled at Bran. "It is nothing, Bran. For a little my brain whirled, but it is gone now. Do not be troubled for me."

"Are you *sure*, Peredur?" Bran asked anxiously and Peredur laughed his great laugh. "I am sure. Do you think I would take chances on the night I stand guard at the door of the treasure?" He held out his arm and Bran laid his own alongside it. "Farewell and farewell, Bran. We shall meet again soon."

"Soon," Bran said, and meant it and went to the door. He stood in the shadow there and watched Peredur take his lance and cross the room to the guard and receive the key and stand at the treasury door. He seemed steady and easy and Bran went to his own quarters and the sleep he needed in preparation for tomorrow's journey.

No one in all the Arch Druid's house was astir when he left. It was yet dark, though the hills above Carleon were outlined with the first misty-white lightening of the predawn. He went rapidly through the sleeping town, marveling again at its size—quite four times as many buildings, he thought, as were in his own village. He passed the last, straggling houses and found the track through the still, vast forest and lengthened his stride. In four days or five, when he had been to Abiris and told him all the tale of his stay with the Arch Druid, he would see Ysobel.

85

Abiris kept him longer at the grove then he had expected, telling again and again each day's small happenings at Carleon. Seven days had passed since his setting out for home before he came to the village in the lake. The news of his coming had run before him and all the people of the village were waiting to welcome him. He saw them crowding the landing when he rounded the curve in the public boat and he was filled with a mixture of pleasure and vexation. He could not but be pleased at this sign of their affection for him, but he had hoped for a quiet meeting with Ysobel.

She was there at the very tip of the landing, her hair blowing in the sharp wind, her face lifted and alight with happiness at seeing him again. Vexation increased in him and he smothered it. They would break away as soon as they could. But first he must return the warm friendliness of the villagers with equal warmth.

He raised his harp in salute as the boatman headed toward the village and the waiting people broke into singing. The boatman brought the dugout to the landing and Carodoc, who had been standing beside Ysobel, reached out a steadying hand and, when Bran had stepped out, pounded his shoulder in welcome while Ysobel took his arm and the crowd shouted, "Hail to Bran the Brave, honored of the Arch Druid above all bards."

The villagers pressed about them as they started toward the town, shouting questions and words of affection, and Bran felt humble and small and unworthy and, at the same time, proud and happy. I might have been gone a year, he thought, and be returning with good news for them. He looked at Ysobel and saw she was aware of his thoughts, and his happiness increased because she knew his heart.

The crowd led them to the center of the village, where a small boy, red-faced with embarrassment and clearly bursting with pride, held a year-old heifer that had been washed and brushed until her shaggy coat gleamed. The oldest man of the tribe made a speech, presenting the heifer to Bran as a sign of their pride and affection for him, and the people began to cheer and stamp their feet.

"HOLD!"

The shout that came from the edge of the group was thin, but it silenced the crowd. They turned as one person toward the sound. A man, a stranger to them all, pushed his way among them. His clothes were soiled and torn and he was drooping with fatigue. His eyes searched the villagers until, seeing Bran's blue robe, he came to him and spoke. "I seek Abiris, the Druid." He staggered a little and Bran caught his arm and Carodoc ran to fetch a horn of mead.

"He is not here, friend. He is three leagues away at the oak grove, where he teaches the young men of the tribe—those who seek knowledge that they may serve Beli and his people." Bran was talking at length to give the man time to collect his strength a little.

Carodoc came with the mead and the stranger drank it gratefully, nodding his thanks but wasting no strength in unnecessary words. "I—must—go—to—him. Will—someone"— he looked at Bran—"set—me—on—my—way?"

"Stay, friend," Bran protested. "You are spent and need rest and food. Come into the house of Abiris and let us refresh you a little before we take you to him. I am Bran the Bard and these are Carodoc and Ysobel, the son and daughter of Abiris."

The stranger shook his head. "I—cannot—stay. I—I—must find Abiris—at—once." His knees sagged and he would have collapsed if it had not been for Bran's support.

"Help me, Carodoc," Bran said and added, to the

stranger, "You cannot go yet, friend. So much is plain. You could not walk a hundred paces without rest. What is it Abiris must know so quickly? Is it"—his voice quickened and deepened with alarm remembering Peredur's talk of marauding Belgae—"is it word of danger from the east?"

The man he was upholding said, "No. It is—the Arch Druid's egg. Stolen."

The crowd gasped and made the sign against evil. They began to press about the man, shouting questions. Bran commanded them, "Back, friends, lest you crush him," and the people moved a little away, muttering. Bran thought he heard someone say "warlock," but he could not be sure and he could not take time now to find the accuser. "Let us get him into the house, Carodoc," Bran said, and Carodoc got his strong arms about the man's waist. Ysobel had already forced her way through the crowd and was running ahead. Bran went before Carodoc, opening a path, and Carodoc half carried the exhausted messenger to the door Ysobel held open.

They laid the stranger on Carodoc's rush bed and Ysobel brought him bread and hot broth. When he had eaten, he made to get up, but Bran pushed him back. "No, you cannot go on. If you will tell me all your message, I will myself take the tale to Abiris. It will reach him more quickly so. Now. Who are you and when did this—this theft take place?" There had been no time for examining the man's message and he wondered now as he waited for the explanation if it were a jest of some kind. No one—no one in his right mind would steal the Arch Druid's bead.

"I am Gaworn of Carleon," the messenger said, "sent by the Arch Druid himself to tell all Druids of the theft of the chevron bead. Eight nights ago, it was."

Ysobel saw Bran's eyebrows jerk up and, counting back

88

over the nights, realized Bran had been still in Carleon eight nights ago.

"*Eight* nights?" Bran's voice was sharp. "You are sure?"

"I am sure," the man said a little sourly.

"But that is impossible. I was myself in Carleon at that time, in the very house of the Arch Druid. I saw the bead and I saw the door that keeps it, locked, and Peredur—Peredur, I tell you, the captain of the guard himself, watching before it."

"That may be. But the following morning, when one came to relieve that same Peredur, the door swung wide, the egg was gone, and Peredur was snoring on the stool before the fire."

"No!" The word came sharp and loud from Bran. "I do not believe it. Peredur would not sleep on guard. Not *Peredur.*"

"So does he say," Gaworn answered. "He says he was given some drug. But none believes him. There was mead still left in his horn and the Arch Druid, willing to trust Peredur, had one of the villeins drink it and the villein suffered no harm."

Bran shook his head in bewilderment. "Then he was ill," he argued, and with the words his face lightened, recalling his parting with his friend. "He *was* ill. I saw him sway upon his feet and begged him to let me call another to stand his watch, but he seemed to recover and answered it was but a momentary swimming in his head, and so I left him."

"He makes no claim to illness," the messenger said and added dryly, "And if he were so ill he could not call out for help, he did recover his health fast enough, for he was well as any man next day, once he'd been shaken awake."

"Yet there must be some way to explain this." Bran was

thinking with distress of the pain that must be even now in Peredur's heart.

"That may be. But none in Carleon believes it. They say Peredur had drunk too much mead from the precious cup he was so proud of and knew not nor cared what happened to the egg. They say someone, coming by in the night, saw him—or heard him snoring, more like—and took the key and stole the egg and went away and Peredur none the wiser. No man thinks *him* a thief—only a man dishonored in his own drunkenness."

Bran said angrily, "Peredur is never drunken," and saw scorn upon Gaworn's face and let it be and asked, "What have they done to him, to my friend Peredur?"

"Not so much," Gaworn answered. "Dismissed him from the guard and sent him from Carleon. I'd have had him in the wicker cage at the Great Circle fire, but it was not for the likes of me to say and the Arch Druid's ever a soft one. No matter. The word must go to Abiris, and if you've a mind to stand here yammering the day through, I'd best be on my way with it."

He passed a hand over his face and stood up, but they could all see his legs tremble. Bran realized he'd forgotten all about Abiris in his distress for Peredur. He must put his friend out of his mind for now. It was obvious the spent messenger would never get to Abiris. He must have run day and night, pausing at every grove to warn each Druid of the theft. He could go no longer without sleep.

"Stay," Bran spoke gently, "until you are truly rested enough to go back to Carleon. Tell the Arch Druid Abiris knows and will make the necessary prayers and sacrifices for the return of the chevron bead and will send the word further to all Druids in this neighborhood."

Listening to him, Ysobel thought he sounded tired and

discouraged, all the happiness and pride of the morning gone
from him, and she could have wept for him, not knowing
all but guessing some of the trouble in his mind. He turned
to Carodoc. "May I take your boat? If Ysobel will come
with me to the further shore and bring it back?" Ysobel
nodded, thinking he had no need to put such a question.
This would give them, at least, a little time together.

They hurried through deserted lanes to the landing. All
the people, Ysobel thought, were inside, talking of the theft,
wondering if it would bring evil to the land, their doors
tight shut against the shadow of evil. Bran had begun to
talk as soon as they were outside, speaking in jerky sentences
about Peredur. "He is a giant of a man, Ysobel. Proud of his
position and absolutely loyal to the Arch Druid. He would
have defended the chevron bead with his life. I'm sure of it.
Something happened beyond his helping it. Something
strange."

They were in the dugout headed for the western shore
of the lake by the time he had finished. Ysobel said, "You
thought him overweary when he came in. Could he, after
you left, have drunk more mead and—and not realized . . ."
Her voice trailed off and he laughed a short, dry laugh.

"Peredur was no puling child, Ysobel. He could drink a
fathom of mead, no matter how weary, and never know
he'd had it. Besides, there was but the one flagon and little
left in it when we two had drunk each a single horn."

"Then he *must* have been drugged as he said."

"How could he have been when the villein who finished
the horn took no harm from what was left?" He frowned.
"Though I would have taken oath he quaffed the full draft
at once—as I did. We were drinking a farewell, Ysobel, not—
not carousing. Still, I did not examine his horn, and I am
likely mistaken. The horn was not empty next day—so I

91

must be. I wish I knew how he is faring. I wish I could find him and tell him I do not believe him false to his trust."

He sounded so forlorn she leaned forward and touched his shoulder and he looked around at her and smiled a little and seemed to take heart from her nearness. "Maybe—maybe it is some foolish person's notion of a jest, my birdling. Maybe the bead has already come home or will do so shortly."

"Maybe," she agreed, not believing it, knowing he did not believe it himself, thanking Beli it was not he on guard that night.

They touched the far bank and he handed her the paddle and scrambled out while she held to a willow already feathered in spring green. "When will you come again, Bran?" she asked wistfully, thinking of their lost day.

"Beli knows, my birdling. I will come as soon as I can, and if I do not come, I shall see you at the Beltane and hold you in my heart the while."

She hoped he could not see the tears that would not stay unshed. The Beltane was so long a time away—nearly three moons—and she felt forlorn and bereft.

CHAPTER SEVEN

Slow time dogged the changing moon and Ysobel set her heart toward Beltane. Bran did not come again to the village in the lake. She could follow him in her mind, for he sent word now and again to tell her what he was doing.

She heard he was deep in his studies of divination and natural philosophy which, when he had completed them, would bring him the green robe of the ovate, the second step upon the way to priesthood. He must work harder than ever now to recover ground lost while he was in Carleon, and he could find no time to leave the teaching grove.

Nevertheless, he did leave, she heard later, under orders from Abiris. Her father, concerned over Bran's worry for Peredur, had sent him to seek his friend. He had as well stayed at the grove, for he had found nothing beyond a rumor that someone had told someone who had told a third that Peredur had been seen at the court of King Cymbeline. Bran had, therefore, returned to the grove and sought to find freedom from worry in his work.

Ysobel saw little of Carodoc during those dragging days. He was busy at his forge from his getting up at dawn to his lying down again, exhausted, as soon as he had eaten a silent meal at night. Ysobel was used to such silences. She guessed he was embarked upon some new design that held his thoughts in thrall. He was not angry or disturbed or sullen, only lost in his own business of creating some beautiful new design for ring or mirror or cup.

The Arch Druid's chevron bead was not found. There were rumors that it had been seen here or heard of there, but each proved false when it was investigated.

There was no more talk of witchcraft. The bustle of spring drew each man to his land, plowing and sowing and watching the weather with far-searching, anxious eyes; or to his flock of sheep and herd of cattle and drove of swine, for among the beasts, too, this was a season of increase. There was no time for idle talk.

Each day the water clock marked more hours of light and everyone's thoughts stretched toward the time of renewing the fires.

Ysobel blessed the need for activity brought by the springing year. She crossed the lake each morning early and called her horse and rode deep into the quiet forest looking for roots and the first spring flowers to pound and boil for dyes or medicines. The wool was taken from the sheep and brought to be carded and dyed and spun ready for the loom. And always there was the pile of damp clay waiting to be made into pots and bowls.

One morning she awoke early, while the villeins still snored, feeling happier than she had since she'd parted from Bran. She lay for a time enjoying a sense of lightness she'd not known for many mornings, not at first bothering to account for it. But as sleep went from her eyes and her muscles, her mind searched for a reason and found it.

Time had ceased to lag. In four days the setting of the fourth moon of the new year would mark the approach of

Beltane and she and Carodoc, with all their household, would go the long journey to the place that was called The Great Hill, where the Beltane would be celebrated. Bran would be there and together they would make their solemn vows of betrothal, at sunset, before the people of Britain, and so end the need to be parted again.

Beside the hearth, Anya rose stiffly and went among the still sleeping figures, nudging and poking them awake. Ysobel sighed and pulled herself from reverie. No wonder she was lighthearted. This was the beginning of the end of waiting.

She yawned and stretched and got up from her bed. These would be long, full days and busy ones and she must be about her work. She thought of all that must be done. Anya meant well, but she was old and the piles of honey cakes for the journey would be spoiled if they were left to her sole care. Meantime, she'd have to see to loading the packhorses. She reached into the big bowl of honey cakes and poured milk into a clay cup and took them with her to the summer cooking fire outside.

They came to The Great Hill that marked the place of the Beltane just as the sun touched the mid-point of the sky dome upon the fourth day after they had set out. Ysobel had pushed Caw ahead of the other horses in her eagerness to see Bran, but she reined in hard now and looked at the color and movement before her.

She had seen the Beltane each spring season for as long as her memory stretched back through her eighteen years. But always, she thought, she forgot the impact of this place and the uncounted people who thronged it. It was, in justice, called the Place of the Mighty Ones. Abiris had told her once it was of great age, though not so ancient as Beli's Circle at the Henge.

The Place of the Mighty Ones had stood, Abiris had said, since a time before the memory of man, a monument to some ancient and forgotten people, two concentric stone rings with an outer circle of a hundred great standing stones. The circles were approached by two avenues lined with pairs of stones different in size and shape, alternating tall and slender and short and squat. Around it, like an emerald torque, setting it apart and protecting it, ran the Wansdyke—a broad ditch cut in the chalky earth, its flat bottom fifty feet below the banks. To right and left and a little away from the circle were low groups of earth mounds and, in the distance, on a line with the mid-point between the avenues, a marvelous high hill. Green trackways, crossing and recrossing the downs in all directions, converged on the Wansdyke, for this shrine belonged, as did the Henge, not to a single tribe but to all the people of Britain.

She wanted to shout aloud in her joy at the scene and would have done so had not Carodoc ridden close to her and leaned across and touched her arm. "Is it not a joy and a wonder, Carodoc?" she asked. "I would not have thought there were so many people in all the world and all of them happy."

Carodoc grinned at her, mocking her enthusiasm a little. "Not all, my sister. There are likely some shaking in their mean little souls, knowing that by this time tomorrow they'll be poorer than they are now, and some who, when the Druids have done their justice, will wish they'd not come to the Beltane."

"Oh, Carodoc, you're nothing but—but a killer of joy."

"Maybe." The laughter went from his face. "But it is well to remember, my sister, the Beltane is not all dancing and leaping and making love. Perhaps we should be as joyful for justice done as for the troths that will be promised. Come, let us find our pavilion, for I am hungry as a starveling wolf with so much riding."

"I want to find Bran," she said, flicking her scarlet leather reins at Caw. "Where will he be, Carodoc, do you know?"

"Patience, Ysobel. You'll not see Bran this day. He will be off yonder." He gestured beyond the mounds to the left of the circle. "Had you forgot our Bran will lead the harping tomorrow and will be at the Druid's quarters now with the other bards? And do you not fret like a young mare at her first bridling. There's enough to see to keep you busy and once we've eaten we'll make a round of the Fair Field. No doubt we'll find some pretty thing for your adorning, for I hear there are traders come with their baubles all the way from Rome itself."

She was disappointed but she had to be content. She *had* forgotten that Bran was to lead the harping and, of course, he would be using every moment to make sure the music went well.

Later, when she walked with Carodoc about the Fair Field, where traders had set out their goods in rough booths of saplings and green boughs, the time passed so quickly she could not believe it when the sun marked the hour for them to go to their pavilion and eat their evening meal and make ready in sleep for the long tomorrow.

They were up before dawn, refreshed and ready for the new day. Ysobel wanted to go again to the traders' booths. She had seen in one of them a string of amber and jet beads. She'd hesitated over buying it, but during the night she'd decided she must have it. It was not so fine in workmanship as the ring Carodoc had made for her, but it would complement the ring. She spoke of it to Carodoc and he agreed she should have it and got from his chest a bridle boss of bronze and blue enamel to give for it in payment.

They did not buy the beads at once, for during the night the Fair Field had filled up with scores of traders who had not been there at sundown and Ysobel must pause to examine all their wares. She saw nothing she liked so much as the jet and amber, but by the time Carodoc had argued the seller into an even trade the sun was nearly half done with its march across the sky. The sellers were closing their stalls and the crowds of people were pushing and scrambling toward the Wansdyke, seeking the best places from which to view the calling down of the fire.

Ysobel pulled the sleeve of Carodoc's tunic, impatient to be off, and Carodoc handed the bridle boss to the trader and received the beads in return. He put them over Ysobel's head and stood back to admire them. "There is time, my sister," he soothed her impatience, and took her arm and led her around the pushing crowd and along one of the trackways that brought them quickly to a place on the very top of the Wansdyke. Trust Carodoc, she thought, to know the best and quickest way anywhere.

The circle of the hundred stones was still empty, but the avenue approaching it from the east was filled with a stately procession. The long, slow-moving line was led by boys in training, their faces and hands and baggy breeches scrubbed and shining. For many of them, the youngest, this was their first Beltane, and Ysobel felt her throat tighten and her eyes dim a little at their solemn, careful faces. One day, in twenty years, many of them would themselves be priests. Behind them came the bards, walking four abreast, carrying their gilded harps and wearing ivy garlands upon their heads. They were followed by the ovates and, finally, the Druids came, two by two, each carrying his spiral-decorated staff, each wearing his great golden torque and, upon his white ceremonial robes, the three rays of light that symbolized the sun. At the very end the Arch Druid walked alone and no eye in the crowd failed to note with sorrow and fear the absence of the chevron bead.

The procession followed the snakelike avenue into the circle, each group taking its set and ordered place about the ring. The Arch Druid approached the altar and held up for all to see a flat, thick disk of glass and began to intone a prayer. His resonant voice carried clear and sharp to every ear in the vast crowd.

> *Grant, O God, Thy protection;*
> *And in protection, strength;*
> *And in strength, understanding;*
> *And in understanding, knowledge;*
> *And in knowledge, the knowledge of justice;*
> *And in the knowledge of justice, the love of it;*
> *And in the love of justice, the love of all existence;*
> *And in the love of all existence, the love of God*
>   *and all goodness.*

The people, who had been still, stirred as the prayer ended and necks craned to get a clearer view of the circle. The Arch Druid lifted the glass disk, turning it a little this way and that until it gathered the sun's rays and directed them upon the pile of dry oak leaves on the altar. Ysobel thought no one among all the waiting thousands drew breath. She found Bran in the forefront of the bards and her heart lifted. A thin curl of smoke drifted up from the leaves and hung a moment in the still air and was gone. There was nothing more for a space of thirty heartbeats; then the whole pile of leaves seemed to burst at once into flame.

The crowd breathed again and the sound was as a little wind in a field of young corn.

Abiris, standing near the altar, handed the Arch Druid two fagots, and he placed them, crossed, over the burning leaves and watched while the fire took them and licked along the outer bark. He stepped back then and a score of the older boys came to the altar and began, carefully, to feed it with other fagots.

The bards raised their harps. The strings flashed like the flashing of lightning in a summer storm. Two hundred hands swept two hundred harps. The Druids began the Deasil Dance, moving in stately measure from east to west about the blazing altar, from which each family here would take home, in a covered pot, new fire for the hearth.

The dance ended and the boys led the re-forming procession toward the western avenue that ended at the Field of the Sanctuary. The crowd had begun to disperse, but Ysobel and Carodoc stayed where they were. Carodoc had chosen their place well, she thought, The marching line would pass close to them. Maybe Bran would look up and give her a sign.

The last of the boys—those who, if Beli willed it, would be bards next Beltane—had gone. The bards were just below her, Bran among them. She had no trouble finding him in the mass of blue robes, for he was a little shorter than most of the others and held himself straighter and more proudly. She willed him to look at her, but she could have saved herself the trouble. He did not so much as turn one eye in her direction. She should have known, she thought, that Bran would not relax until he had come to the Sanctuary Field.

She'd go after him, along the edge of the avenue, outside

the sacred stones, and find him there waiting. He would be expecting her.

"Let us go, Carodoc," she said to her brother. "I want to see Bran."

Carodoc checked her with his hand. "Stay, Ysobel. You cannot go yet. It would not be seemly to leave until the Arch Druid has passed. Bran will not run away."

She did not argue. Carodoc was right, of course. They were conspicuous on this high bank and their going would be noted. A Druid's son and daughter could not risk an act of discourtesy to the Arch Druid. She watched the rest of the procession without interest. She wished they would hurry, but they walked as if there were no end to time. When the Arch Druid had gone two paces beyond their lookout point, she said, "Now, Carodoc. Hurry," and he laughed at her. "Come then, oh soul of impatience, I know a secret and quick path. We'll likely be at the Field of the Sanctuary before your Bran."

But others had learned Carodoc's secret and the path was choked with families and friends of bards and ovates anxious to greet their own. When they came to the field there was no sign of Bran. Ysobel darted about like a butter-fly and Carodoc was hard put to it to keep her in sight. He saw Abiris, standing near the sanctuary stone, and called over half a dozen heads, "Wait, Ysobel. Yonder's our father."

Ysobel stopped where she was and waited for him to come up to her. "Use your head to save your heels, sister," he said. "Abiris stands near the sanctuary. He will, of a certainty, know where to find Bran."

"Why, then, do we stay here chattering?" Ysobel asked tartly, and he made a gesture of mock despair and guided her through the crush of people.

Abiris stood, in a little clear space, protected from the pushing and jostling by his Druid's robe and tonsure. He was, Ysobel thought, enjoying the bustle about him—the laughter and the shouts of greeting, the snatches of singing, and the occasional rings of dancers who were already beginning the merrymaking. Her heart caught at the wistfulness she saw in his face and she wondered if he would not like to lay aside his robe and with it the dignity and reserve expected of a Druid and for once make merry himself. She saw him then as she had never seen him before, as a human being like herself, not as her father, who had loved her and disciplined her all her life, or as a stern and upright judge, or as a teacher sworn to pass his knowledge and experience to younger men that the tribe might prosper, or even as a priest whose life was dedicated to the service of the god. She wondered what manner of man lay under these things and what he had been like as a boy and how he had felt when he first put on a bard's robe. She called out to him, "Father," but he did not answer, probably did not hear her.

At the moment of her call a single figure—a plain figure in dark-plaid trousers and leather jerkin, an anonymous, ordinary man—whirled from a singing group, thrust something into Abiris' hand, and whirled away again to be lost at once in the crowd. She saw Abiris look around, startled, then down at the thing he held, before another group of dancers hid him from her.

"What was that?" Carodoc asked, and she thought he was worried or distressed. "I'm afraid it means trouble, whatever it is. People do not, usually, approach a priest without ceremony, not even at the Beltane."

He was pushing among the people, using his elbows to demand a path, since words were lost at once in the hubbub.

She went after him, puzzled, thinking there was little need for worry. Anything could happen at the Beltane. Perhaps the plain dark man had used this means to offer a new song for the singing of the bards.

The look upon her father's face when they came near him warned her she was wrong. There *was* trouble—serious trouble. He stood as if he had caught a buffet—pain and dismay in his look. His shoulders drooped and the hand that held a piece of smooth gray birchbark trembled.

Carodoc reached him first and laid an arm about the drooping shoulders. When he spoke his voice was low and troubled. "Father. Father, what is it?"

Abiris looked at him as if he were a stranger and held out to him the birchbark and Ysobel, beside him now, saw the hatched marks of a message upon it. She took the bark and peered at it, glad her father had taught her long ago to know the letters of their little-used alphabet. Carodoc had never learned them, she thought idly, having as he said no need for writing and no time to learn it. She wondered why she thought of such trifles now and knew she was trying to push away from her the shock of the words she was reading, to keep her mind from accepting what her eyes had seen.

"What *is* it, Ysobel?"

She read slowly, not knowing her face mirrored the face of Abiris, "Bran the Bard is a warlock. He has bewitched men and animals and crops. He stole . . ." Her voice broke off and she looked at her brother stupidly.

"Well? *Finish* it, Ysobel!"

She began again jerkily. "He stole—— Oh, *Carodoc*. It says he stole the Arch Druid's egg. And—it says—at the end—justice!"

Carodoc snatched the bark from her and held it before his eyes as if the very need to see for himself could teach him, on the instant, the meaning of the marks. He said, "This is—this is absurd. You misread the writing, Ysobel. You must have. Bran . . ."

Ysobel did not hear him. She had turned to Abiris. "Where is he, father?" she asked. "Where is Bran?"

The sound of her words cut through the daze that held Abiris. He snapped his shoulders straight and took the bark from Carodoc with a hand that was as steady as the standing stones in the circle. "No." The word was a command from Abiris, the Druid, Priest of Beli and Judge of the Law.

"But, father. I must find him. At once. You see that."

"You will not seek him, Ysobel. I command it. Carodoc, you will see that your sister obeys my command." He looked from one to the other and saw her hurt and anguish and felt them as his own and gentled his voice. He looked down at the message and frowned and spoke more softly. "This —this accusation—it is a vile thing, secretly made and secretly given to me. But it is, for all that, a serious charge, my daughter, and it must be treated in the manner proper to such charges. The fact that it is made against Bran does not change my—my duty. I must question him as I would question any stranger."

"But, father, you cannot believe that *Bran*——"

"Believe?" he interrupted her. "It is not for me to believe or disbelieve. I am Druid and Judge, an instrument for the will of Beli and the laws of this land. It is my duty to question Bran and I will not have you interfering with my duty. I cannot let you go running to warn him. He must come to me as any other man would come and hear what his unknown accuser has to say and answer it."

"But, father," she began again and he held up his hand for silence and spoke reasonably. "Do you not see, Ysobel, that this is needful? Needful for *Bran's* own sake. Whatever happens, I must take this matter to the Arch Druid. The whole order is to consider, at the judging time, the matter of the theft and hear what has been done from the Arch Druid himself. It may be—it likely is true that some other such message has been handed to some other of the Druids. Do you not see that I must be able to say to the Arch Druid—to them all —that I have myself questioned Bran? Do you not see I must be able to say upon my oath before Beli that Bran came to me without prior warning, without time to prepare a defense against these charges? I have no doubt that he will answer them quickly and completely and that will be an end to it. But he must not be warned. He must be treated as any other man accused of dishonoring the god by thievery. No one must be able to say he had special treatment because of me."

She saw the point of his thinking and nodded slowly in agreement. "Then do you send for him quickly that we may quickly hear his defense and be done with it."

"We? No, Ysobel. Not we. You and Carodoc will leave here at once. What must take place is between Bran and me. When he has cleared himself I will send him to you."

Her quick anger rushed at her. Why was he so—so cruel? What touched Bran touched her, for before this day was done they would be betrothed. Abiris had no right to keep her from her beloved in a time of trouble. She stamped her foot upon the hard ground. "I will *not* go."

"You will go, Ysobel, for I, Abiris the Druid, do so order it in the name of Beli." He turned from her and waited for the sound of her going, but she did not move and he said roughly, over his shoulder, "Must I summon the guard to have you taken by force?"

Carodoc put his arm about her. "Come, Ysobel. Come and do not fear. Bran will answer these charges and all will be well. It is only for a little time. But you must leave. Now."

He led her away, toward the place of their pavilion, and she went, not knowing what else to do, in anger and hurt and uncertainty at the words of Abiris, her father—but a Judge.

CHAPTER EIGHT

BRAN went from the lighting of the new fire in the circle straight on past the Field of the Sanctuary to the Druid's quarters. He wanted to change his ceremonial clothes for his ordinary blue robe and leave his harp where it would be safe. His duties for the day were over and he was free to find Ysobel and spend with her the time between now and sunset, when they would go to the edge of the circle and, before Abiris and all the people of Britain, give their troth each to the other.

The ceremony had lifted his heart and resolved, to some degree again, the doubts of his faith that had renewed themselves in his mind after the theft of the Arch Druid's bead. During the slow nights that had dragged their length from his home-coming to the Beltane his heart had veered as a weathercock between his old, firm belief in all he had been taught and the new fear that Beli was but a story made by the Druids for the sake of their own power. But today the music and prayers and the awe-filled moment when the Arch Druid had called down the new fire had purged his bitter doubting and he felt renewed in faith and light as the air about him.

His mind was busy with plans for the day as he came to

the stone house where the bards and ovates were quartered each Beltane. Elaine, the old woman who cared for the place, hobbled out of the shadows of the long common room to meet him. He remembered the first time he had seen her when he had come, as a boy of ten, to his first Beltane, proud and full of awe and a little frightened. She had taken charge of him and cleansed his face and hands from the dust of the trackway and brushed his breeches and tunic and told him not to fear. He had only to walk straight, she had promised, and keep his hands still and do as he was told and before he knew it he would be a man grown and a bard as well.

She met him now as she had met him every year since his first coming and fussed over him and scolded him when he would have hurried to his changing. He told her of Ysobel, waiting for him on the Field of the Sanctuary, and she nodded her gray old head and said it was time they two were made one and straightened his robe and promised to keep his harp safe for him. He left the stone house at last with her blessings in his ears and almost ran straight into one of the boys from the lake village coming fast to the lintel.

"Beli keep you, Bran the Bard," the boy said.

Bran answered automatically, a little irritated at even this small further delay, "And you, Prydain," and would have hurried on, but the boy laid a hand on his arm and stopped him.

"Wait, Bran. I bring you a message from Abiris, the Druid. He bids you come to him on the Field of the Sanctuary."

"Now?" Bran wondered what Abiris wanted with him.

"At once. I am to bring you straightly to him."

"What does he want?" Bran sounded testy. He would

never get to Ysobel at this rate and she must be fretting, being never one to bear waiting patiently.

"I do not know. He stopped me as I was hurrying past and bade me seek you here and bring you. His face was black as any crow and I did not stay to question though I have my own business to hurry toward."

Ysobel! Bran thought. Something is wrong with Ysobel and he said, "Hurry then," to Prydain, and started off at such a pace the boy had to run to keep up with him.

Prydain did not stay when they came to Abiris. He ran quickly off before he could be stopped again and Bran, forgetting to approach the Druid with the formality due from a bard, said roughly, "Ysobel?"

Abiris stared at him, displeased at the lack of ceremony. These young men, he thought, were all alike, without proper respect for their elders. Even Bran, whom he had thought so different from the rest. He wanted to keep this meeting upon a formal base. It was hard enough that he must face any bard with charges of sorcery and theft without having Bran stressing their personal relationship. He looked sternly at Bran and did not answer his question.

Bran did not see the disapproving look. "Where is she?" He took Abiris' arm and shook it. "What has happened to her? Is she ill? *Tell* me. Tell me quickly."

Abiris freed his arm from Bran's grasp. "Control yourself, Bard, and mind your tongue. You forget to whom you speak."

Bran felt as if he had been immersed in icy water, but he had to know about Ysobel. "Where is Ysobel, Abiris? You must tell me."

"Ysobel is in her pavilion. There is nothing wrong with her. Will you——"

Bran interrupted, relief mixing with irritation and making him doubly careless in his manner, "Then what is all this—this formality and rebuking? Why have you sent for me, Abiris? I have finished my duties. The rest of the day should be mine as you promised."

Abiris held out the piece of birchbark and his voice thundered, "Be quiet, Bard, and read." He waited, watching Bran's face, his own cold and proud and distant.

Bran read the words on the bark.

> *Bran the Bard is a warlock. He has bewitched*
> *men and animals and crops. He stole the Arch*
> *Druid's egg. He is, therefore, also a thief.*
> *He must be punished. Justice. Justice. Justice.*

He finished the reading and looked at Abiris and laughed. He saw Abiris stiffen and saw a look of trouble and doubt come into his face. He heard Abiris' voice and his words rebuking the laughter. "This is not a matter for amusement, Bran the Bard."

Bran flicked the birchbark with his finger. "But it is, Abiris. What else? Are you tired or ill? What could such nonsense be but a jest, even though a poor one? *I* a warlock? *I* steal the Arch Druid's egg? Whoever wrote this must be witless."

"You think charges of witchcraft and sacrilegious theft matters for jesting, Bard? Think again."

Abiris took the birchbark out of Bran's hand and tucked it beneath the golden belt that circled his robe. He did not relax the stern and stiff set of his mouth and Bran felt the beginning of uncertainty and the laughter, still lingering in his mind, died.

"You surely do not believe me guilty of such things, Abiris?" His pride was hurt and he was stung by the rebuke and the manner of Abiris and he knew his voice lacked in respect but he could not help it.

"Did you steal the Arch Druid's bead, Bard?"

Bran felt insulted by the question and by Abiris' constant use of *Bard* as if he were just any bard, not like a son to this man. He was hurt and angered beyond reason that Abiris should feel the need to put such a question to him. Abiris knew his heart and mind. He must know him incapable of sorcery and theft. He said, "Need you ask *me* such a question, Abiris? Need you insult me in this manner?" and closed his lips stubbornly, too proud to deny what was so obviously a lie.

"Did — you — steal — the — Arch — Druid's — chevron — bead?" Abiris set each word apart from the next, ignoring Bran's questions, watching his face with untrusting eyes.

Bran would not speak. He told himself he would not lower himself to answer the question. Let Abiris think what he would.

Abiris waited and the two stood silent, scowling at each other, until something in the face of Abiris, something implacable and demanding, told Bran he *must* answer, told him his own pride was not shield enough against the will of the Druid. He shouted in anger, "NO!" and, again, "NO!" and saw his denial heard with disbelief. He could not, he would not, accept the disbelief. His mind sought excuses for Abiris. He must be tired. He was getting old. His mind was not as clear as it used to be. Left alone he would come to his own proper senses before sunset. He asked, "And now have I your leave to go?"

Abiris said, "No," sharply, and Bran looked at him, defiant, thinking he would go without leave then and knowing he dare not unless he were willing to forfeit his bardship. Abiris was a Druid and his word was law. For the

first time Bran found himself hating his foster father and
the power in him and fearing him.

Abiris put up his hand and rubbed his head, aching
with his emotions. He could read Bran's thoughts clearly
enough and he could not believe that this angry, defiant,
shouting man was his beloved foster son. When he had
seen Bran coming with the boy he had felt some relief
from the tension that had been building in him while he
waited. He would show him the birchbark and Bran would
explain quickly and easily, would offer proof he could
not have been the thief. For the other charge, the charge of
witchcraft, Abiris was not troubled. Such charges were
frequently made and had only to be investigated a little
to be proven false. Doubtless special cases of sorcery would
be somehow brought to his attention later and he could
himself show they were false. Bran was no warlock.
So much he knew. But the charge of theft was a different
case. And now Bran was behaving as—as a guilty man
might in truth behave. The simple denial—without explanation, without proof—spoken in anger and defiance. What
was the boy thinking of? *Was* he, then, in truth a thief
and hoped to brazen out the charge?

Bran waited, glaring, his hands picking at his robe, while
Abiris searched his memory for all he had heard of the
theft. What, he wondered, had the Arch Druid discovered
by his questioning at Carleon? He would hear later in the
day, but he had best have the story again from Bran. The
whole story of the day of the theft.

He drew in his breath, conscious that he was tired and
sick in his spirit. "Do you, Bran, tell me of your last day
and night in Carleon. Tell me everything you said and
did, hour by hour. Leave nothing out."

Bran said, trying to be reasonable, "But all that is four

moons gone, Abiris. I cannot remember it all. Besides, you heard it from me when it was fresh. I told you over and over when I came back to the grove."

"No matter. Tell it again."

Why won't he believe me? Bran thought. What have I done to set him against me? Hurt and anger twisted his heart. He tried to remember what he had said when he first came home from Carleon. Suppose the story as he retold it varied in some detail? Would Abiris seize upon this as proof of his guilt since he seemed so willing to believe him a thief? He wanted to cry out these things to Abiris. He wanted to refuse this order, to smile and say, "What has come between us that you have lost your trust in me and I feel in my heart hatred and fear of you?" but the steady hardness in the face before him was a barrier between them and under the unwavering, cold look he heard himself telling what he had been commanded to tell.

When he had done, Abiris said, "Again," and Bran went back and retold the story and retold it, wearily and protesting, yet a third time. He resented each word and he grew more and more afraid as he knew he was halting and stumbling over words that should have come smoothly to his lips, mixing himself up because he was bewildered and heartsick and alone.

He came to the end for the third time and Abiris felt as if he were smothering in a dark and ugly cloud that was shutting him away from Beli's face forever. He had been loathe to take up the accusation with Bran, since he had no liking for unsigned writings. He had seen the messenger but briefly, but even in the one quick look he had recognized him as a sometime companion of Evelake, and Abiris had no trust for Evelake. But Abiris the Druid could not fail to summon any man so accused. He had, after the first shock, had little fear for Bran's denial. Sending Prydain had been little more than a gesture, but a gesture that must be gotten over with as quickly as possible so that the message could be forgotten and all of them get along with the business and pleasure of the Beltane.

So he had thought. But Bran—his dearly loved Bran— had blustered and laughed where he should have denied and given proof of innocence. And now—now he had told his story three times and no two times alike. More, he had failed in respect to Abiris the Druid and Abiris, touched alike in his pride and his love, must believe his foster son guilty. So be it. He took Bran by the arm and shook him and said, with anger and disappointment and something that was close to bitter hating, "Hear me now and I will show you what must be the truth."

He took, then, the jagged pieces of that day and night and put them together into a new tale. He said he must suspect, since Bran could not tell a simple story three times the same, that Bran had drugged Peredur's drinking horn, the horn that everyone knew for its silver bosses; that Bran had left the room of the treasure and hidden himself in the shadows and watched until Peredur slept deeply; that Bran had stolen again into the room and taken the key to the treasury and seized the chevron bead and gone to his rest.

Bran heard him and wondered desperately how to counter suspicion with nothing more than words, though he knew them in his own heart to be all true. He fought creeping dismay and gathered his wits for argument and tried to speak carefully and calmly for his very life.

"There was no drug in the mead found next day in the horn."

"No, for you took care to cleanse the horn and pour into

it a little fresh mead. Since you were drinking farewell the one to the other, Peredur would have left no mead in the horn, and this you must know."

"Where would I get this drug you speak of?"

Abiris laughed, but the laugh was bitter and scornful. "Every bard knows there is a store of such drugs wherever there are Druids. You had many days to search out the Arch Druid's simples and take what you needed."

Bran felt as if he had himself been drugged. He searched his mind for another argument and found it. "What of the scar-faced guard? Did he stand watching while I dropped poison into Peredur's horn?"

Abiris' answer was full of contempt. "Even the boys of eleven winters have learned at the teaching groves the skills of the hand. Would you have me think you, a bard, so lacking in elementary muscular control that you cannot drug a drinking horn unseen? Had the guard been beside you instead of across a shadow-filled room you could still have made the mead foul and he no wiser."

Bran gave up then. He was too exhausted of mind and too ill of heart to argue. He could not think, though he knew he must. Abiris believed him a thief. Abiris had not called him warlock yet, but likely he believed that, too. There was a certain logic in the things Abiris had said. Only they were not true. So much he knew. But there was no witness to declare upon his oath that the tale Abiris had told was false. There was no way he could fight phantoms, not with Abiris before him, withdrawn from him, distrusting him, hating him. There was nothing more he could do here. He would ask again for permission to go and hope that a little time would change Abiris. He lifted his head and saw Abiris with face crumpled in pain and sorrow and eyes filling with tears.

"Bran, Bran," Abiris said. "I am an old man and I have loved you as a son for all the years of your life. I have no heart to denounce you to the Arch Druid. If you will but return the bead, return it secretly, before sunset and leave, of your own will, the company of the bards, I will destroy this writing and keep your secret in my heart forever."

Bran thought he had known all possible emotions during his interview with Abiris, but he found now he heard Abiris—offering to destroy the writing if he would return the bead—with shock and a kind of disgust. This, he thought, was not what he would have expected of Abiris. If Abiris truly believed him guilty of these crimes, then Abiris should not have hesitated to perform his own duty. Abiris was a Druid, a keeper of the good for all the people, not—not a simple man with the right to forget his obligations even for a moment. Bran felt a different kind of bitterness and out of it spoke bitterly. "I am kin-shattered, Abiris the Druid. As well for me to die—even as a warlock in the fires of the Henge under the full moon—as be doomed to the death in life of a man landless and cattleless, a fugitive from the company of Beli's Priests, forced to wander alone for unknown years, a beggar or, at best, a trickster at the fairs. I say again I had no part in the theft of the Arch Druid's chevron bead. If you will not believe me, do you at least go and do your duty."

He saw Abiris harden his heart, saw his face tighten again into sternness and contempt and shame because he had shown Bran his weakness. "So be it, Bard. I have given you a chance. I will go now to the Arch Druid."

"It may be you will find the Arch Druid wiser and kinder than you. It may be you will find *he* has already discovered the true thief."

"It may be. I doubt it. If he had caught the thief, I should have been told. For your part, do not leave the place of the

Beltane. Hold yourself ready for the command of the Order of the Druids and may Beli help you."

Bran thought, I cannot leave him so. I cannot, no matter what he is or what he thinks. He has been as my father. He said, "Abiris. Abiris, I . . ." But Abiris turned away from him, not listening, without a word or a look of kindness or love or pity, without one sign of trust, and walked from him. Bran watched him go until he could no longer see him and turned and ran from the place as if it were infested with spirits.

CHAPTER NINE

BRAN stumbled among the people of Britain as his mind stumbled among its broken thoughts.

He would go away from here. He would go to Cymbeline and find Peredur and . . . Abiris had forbidden him to go—anywhere. But he must not stay. If he stayed, they would bring him to the Justices. He could—he could vanish in the crowd and. . . . He had no clothes for vanishing. The blue robe. . . . (This was the Beltane—the time of happiness.) The blue robe. His bard's robe and the tonsure. They would mark him wherever he went. (Ysobel. He must find Ysobel.) Abiris would send the guard after him if he tried. . . .

He must order his mind. He must—somehow—achieve calm and logic to think what he could do to save himself, what he could say to the Order of the Druids when they sent for him and named him thief. He forced himself to repeat the triads he had learned and loved, those groups of three that set forth the aspirations and the beliefs of the people and Beli's laws of beauty in the soul of man and in the world. They had never failed heretofore to renew his strength and calm him.

They failed him now. They seemed now without meaning and substance, mocking his new-found faith.

Ysobel . . . the Arch Druid's bead . . . Peredur! If he could only find Peredur. But none knew where he had gone. The wicker cage for the burnt offering to Beli. (Warlock. Warlock. Warlock.) He must find Ysobel. Ysobel said the Tor was not an evil place. But it was. It was. They should not have climbed it. Had it not been for Joshua ben Joseph. . . . Your friend, Ysobel, not mine. . . . Seek truth, he had said, that strange, quiet man. Seek truth and if you find it, if you know it, truth will free you from all evil.

Truth will free you from all evil.

His mind steadied. The changing, falling, tumbling thoughts took on form and order. He could think again.

What was he to do? How could he disprove the lying charges upon the birchbark. Abiris had not clearly seen the man—the ordinary, anonymous man—who had thrust the message at him. Then who had written it? There were not so many who knew the secret of writing. If he could discover. . . .

Truth. Find the truth and know it and it will set you free.

"Do you suppose truth lies at the bottom?" Ysobel had asked once as they had leaned idly above the two-chambered Druid's well at Ynis Witrin and seen the stars reflected in its depth though it was yet daylight. His truth, the truth about the Arch Druid's bead, did not lie at the bottom of a well, but it must be somewhere. Someone stole the jewel. No doubt someone had drugged Peredur's mead and washed the horn and put fresh mead into it, just as Abiris had told it. Who? There had to be an answer, for he knew he had done no more than touch the bead once, reverently, for luck. He would have to find the thief.

Find the thief. That must come first. Then he would be free to disprove the charges of witchcraft.

Free? But would he be free? How long would he be free to do anything? If he were truly suspected of witchcraft and thievery, would they not seize him and hold him in Carleon until the time for his destruction? How *then* find the truth? Or try to find it?

He beat his forehead with his two clenched fists and cried out his despair and felt a hand upon his arm and looked for the first time with eyes that saw what was before them and said, "Ysobel," in a terrible voice.

"He didn't believe you," she said bleakly, and he answered as bleakly, "You know."

She nodded and said no more and took his arm and led him a little away to her own pavilion. It was empty and they sat upon a pile of rushes and she said, "Tell me, Bran. From the beginning. Everything you remember," and he began, "Someone wrote on birchbark——"

She broke in upon him. "Not that. I know that. I was there and saw the writing. Tell me of Carleon."

He wanted to protest and did not, so grateful for her trust he would not deny her anything, though he thought another telling would but cause him to retch. He told it, wearily, and completely. He spoke of Evelake, and she said sharply, "Evelake! Evelake was in Carleon?"

He read her mind and smiled thinly and said, "Let him be, Ysobel. He *had* been there, but he had gone to take Ganhelon's hunting dogs to Brittany, gone the evening before the bead was stolen. Besides, he is the old Evelake again and done with foolhardiness."

She listened quietly then to the end, careful to hide her quick-killed hope that Evelake was the thief. When he had done she said, "What can we do?"

"Find the truth," he answered with more assurance than he felt, though being with her, seeing her steadfast courage and faith in him had raised his spirits. "Since I did not take the bead and it is gone, someone else did. I must find him."

"Yes. We must find him. But first we must get you away. You cannot search out the truth from"—her voice stumbled over the words, but she made herself speak them—"from a wicker cage in Carleon."

"I cannot run away." He gestured to his blue robe. "This and my tonsure will betray me and I have no other clothes."

She was at the end of the pavilion stuffing food into a pack. "No, but you can lie close in the forest nearby until I send you breeches and a plain dun cloak. When your hair has grown again over the tonsure—and it will not take long —no one will recognize you, not if you are careful. Hurry now. It is almost sunset and I doubt not they will send to find you once the last judgment has been given."

"Ysobel this is—is dangerous. They will know you helped me and you will suffer for it."

"Peace, Bran." She went to the pavilion opening and looked out. "No one knows you have been here. No one will guess. I shall tell them I have not seen you, that I was at the Fair Field getting a new necklace." She touched the jet and amber at her throat. "Carodoc will know, but he will stand by me. Only hurry, Bran. *Hurry.*"

He took the pack from her. He had not the heart to argue further. Maybe she was right. Maybe this was the only way to find the truth. She went before him, her eyes sharp for sight of a familiar face in the dancing, singing throng. She had no time for thinking or for weeping over their broken happiness. That could come later. Now she must get him safe away, quickly away, before they sent to seize him, but not so quickly as to attract attention.

122

He was lagging behind her and she waited and when he had come beside her took his arm and looked into his face. They were nearly to the edge of the field. The first of the forest trees cast long, welcoming shadows toward them. But there were still people about and she had caught one or two of them looking at Bran's face. It wouldn't do to have them remembering the gaunt, frightened look of it.

"Try to look more cheerful, Bran. Try to pretend. . . ." She saw his look that had been seeking to do as she bade him change and felt him tense. She turned quickly and saw what he had seen and felt a sudden push and was lying upon her back in an oak grove seeing Bran going quickly away from her toward a squad of archers led by two men with bare swords. She called, "Bran," and he did not answer but made a flat, chopping motion with his hand behind his back and she understood it was a sign to silence her. She started to call to him again and checked herself. He was right. If she were suspected of helping him—trying to help him—to escape, Abiris would set a guard upon her. She must be free to seek Bran's truth for him. She got up slowly from the ground and saw the pack of food where he had dropped it beside her and picked it up, holding it awkwardly before her.

He was walking toward the archers. When he came to them he held out his hands and the captain of the squad bound them together with a leather thong. The sun, sinking as her heart was dying, shone into Bran's face and he turned a little toward where she was hidden and, lifting his bound hands, spelled out in the finger alphabet they had learned together from Abiris the word "truth."

One of the archers jerked at him and turned him from her and she saw his whole body sag in discouragement. The sword-bearers, side by side, stepped out briskly toward the stone circle. Against the darkening sky the rekindled sacred fire danced bright upon the altar, but to her it seemed no longer an omen of a new day but rather of a doom that would end Bran's life.

The leader of the guard struck Bran between his bowed shoulders and he stumbled a little. Then, as if some new strength had come into him with anger at the blow, he straightened his body and, proud and erect, walked steadily between the swordsmen and the archers.

She watched until she could no longer see him clearly, then went slowly back toward her pavilion, not knowing or caring that all around her the great bonfires that would last through half the night were already beginning to burn in the dusk. There would be no dancing and singing for her this night, no laughter as the young men of Britain leaped their great leaps over the leaping flames. She had forgotten that this was the Beltane, the joyous festival of new fires and new crops and the plighting of troths. Her heart was darker than the coming night. She came to the pavilion and lay upon the rushes and wept until she had no more tears.

Abiris found her there, lying still and desolate. He saw her upon the rushes by the ghost reflection of the great fires that rose and fell upon the thin cloth walls. He stood just within the tent opening and said, "Ysobel," and his voice was old and empty and pitiful, but she did not answer him. He came toward her and looked down at the bed of rushes and waited. He waited a long time and she did not stir or look at him and he said again, "Ysobel," and she answered him at last out of her aching misery, "Go away."

He flinched as if she had struck him. "I will not go,

Ysobel. Do you think my sorrow less than yours? Do you think Bran has been less dear to me than you and Carodoc? That he would steal——"

"No!" She got up from the rushes and stood before him, anger and hatred blazing in her and giving her a new life. "Why do you say such things? You know the mind and heart of Bran the Brave. You know he is—is as true to Beli and to Beli's laws as—as you yourself."

He held up his hand. "No man knows the mind and heart of another," but she would not hear him and rushed on with her own talking. "Test him. Test Bran. What does your own law say? 'In three things will be seen the soul of a man. In what he may fear. In what he would conceal. In what he would show.' Does Bran fear anything save wrong thinking and wrong doing? Does he conceal anything? Does he show anything but gentleness and faith to Beli and a—a burning will to serve the god and the people? You cannot— you dare not answer otherwise."

He said angrily, "Be quiet, girl! Do not tell me what I do and do not dare. You are ill with grief for Bran and your wits have left you. I am Abiris the Druid. Hear me now."

He told her things she knew and things she did not— things he had learned this day since he had talked to Bran. He told her the Arch Druid had ordered an investigation that included everyone who had been in his house or had the opportunity to be there on the day of the theft. They were all accounted for, innocently accounted for, except one disgruntled villein who had run away some time later as he had often vowed to do. Only Bran could be guilty. Only he could not explain his actions to everyone's satisfaction. Only he had been in the room with an opportunity to drug Peredur's horn. No one else could have stolen into the locked treasury and taken the egg. There was no room, no possible room for doubt.

She said, stung at last to speech, "Evelake?" and he frowned at her. "Do you not think I have considered Evelake? No man guesses his mind and heart and there have been disturbing tales about him. But Evelake was not there."

"He was in Carleon. He talked to Bran."

"Yes. But not on the night of the theft. He talked to others, too, many of them, and there are those in Carleon who have taken their oaths before Beli they saw him upon his way with Annwyn, his shadow, full six and twenty hours before the theft could have been accomplished. And there are others to tell of the food he bought for a long journey. It was not Evelake, Ysobel."

Her eyes flickered as she saw a thin thread of hope. They could have come back, Evelake and Annwyn. The buying of food could have been a ruse. If only it were possible to find proof of that. But the Druids would not seek it, she thought bitterly. They were satisfied Bran was the thief and would not look further. Bran had been right. They were evil men seeking only their own ends. If she could find the proof. But she was only a woman and she doubted if she could succeed where the Arch Druid had failed. Or . . .

"Only Bran is left." She heard the shaking of her father's voice and knew he was sick with pain at what he thought Bran had done, but there was no pity in her. "That is not true," she insisted stubbornly.

He made a hopeless gesture, but he did not argue. "There is, too, the charge of witchcraft."

The charge of witchcraft. How could she have forgotten it? But she had. The shadow of the wicker cage and Bran within it grew in her mind and shut out the rushlight and the reflection of the leaping fires and all her power to think.

Abiris said, "Ysobel!" sharply as if he had cracked a leather whip in her ear and the shadow went away and she got up from the earth. She stood above him and her voice rang harsh as iron on stone in the pavilion. "*You* are bewitched if you believe such a thing. There is no evil in Bran, neither of thievery nor of witchcraft. He is free from evil and as true as a little child. I will show you"—she thought of Bran's bound hands spelling out the word truth—"even I, Ysobel, a lone woman, will show all of you. I will find the truth and I will bring it to you and I will never again . . ."

"Then," he interrupted harshly, "you must find it quickly, for Bran will be brought to judgment at midsummer at Beli's Henge."

She looked at him and did not see him. She had thought to have more time. Midsummer. Scarce fifty nights hence. Less than two moons.

Abiris was still speaking and his words broke through her fear and despair. ". . . do not believe Bran is a warlock. I will myself search out those men and animals and crops said to be bewitched to find the witch marks upon them. If I prove those charges false, he will not suffer burning. So much I can do and will do for the memory of Bran the Brave, my nearly son. But he will die, Ysobel, for the theft of the chevron bead and for sacrilege. You must not hope otherwise."

She did not answer him. She picked up the wolfskin from her rush bed, remembering the night would be chill and she must keep her body strong for helping Bran, and with it on her arm went out into the flame-decked night. She heard her father calling her, begging her to come back, brokenly, like a whimpering, hurt hound, but she did not heed his call. She walked steadily through the laughing, singing, dancing, leaping world of the Beltane as if she were an unseen soul until she left it behind her and came to an ancient mound of earth and lay down at its foot and wrapped herself in the skin.

CHAPTER TEN

Carodoc found her there in the white, swirling fog of dawn, her hair snarled and drenched with mist, her body curled for warmth inside the wolfskin. He had been seeking her for hours, since, at midnight, he had come in from watching the Beltane merrymaking and found Abiris bowed in despair beside a guttering rushlight and heard, hurriedly, his story and learned that Ysobel had left the pavilion. He had gone at once to the place where they had tethered the horses and found her gelding and thought she could not have gone far, alone and on foot.

He had searched for her among the great fires, among the young men and women who still danced and leaped and sang, among the lonely and deserted booths of the Fair Field, empty now of their bright wares and forlorn. He had searched slowly, methodically, in widening circles from the pavilion, berating himself that he had left Ysobel when he had led her away from Abiris, being so sure there had been no danger to Bran, that Bran would give quick proofs of his innocence to Abiris.

Carodoc did not believe Bran was a warlock, did not believe he had stolen the bead. Bran, for all his strength and his mighty voice and his good, solid brain, was little more than a lad. The strength of his mind, through perception of the world and knowledge of the hearts of men and women and the great, stalking evil that was as much a part of living as the beauty and good Bran believed in, could grow to match his physical manhood. But now he was simple and believing, trusting all things and all men. It would not, Carodoc was sure, have come into his mind that anyone, least of all himself, could do such evil as steal a thing sacred to the worship of the god he served. His reverence for Beli was a white flame pointing toward the sun. His pursuit of the service of the god was single-minded. And, Carodoc thought wryly, even if Bran had coveted the jewel, he would not have had the guile to spin so neat a web of deceit to get it. Such planning was more—Carodoc's face, unseen in the dark by the people about him, carried upon it the mark of pain his thoughts brought him—more like Evelake.

Where *was* Evelake? He had not been at the Beltane or, if he had been, he had taken pains to keep himself hidden. But there was nothing so strange in that. Evelake would not, likely, want to come to the first great festival since his failing the test, the first festival in which he should have taken part as a bard. But where had he been in all the long days since Bran had spoken to him at Carleon? No one had seen him at the village, for Carodoc had inquired. No one seemed to know where he had gone. Carodoc sighed. Here was another mystery and he had no stomach for more unknown things. He would try to find out later. There was no time to solve this small problem now.

Something had happened to Evelake since he had been banished from the Druid Order. He had been willful always, impatient and sometimes thoughtlessly cruel in planning the jests he delighted in. But he had been no more than thoughtless. Now, since his expulsion from the teaching groves, he had changed. He, too, seemed to be lit by a flame, but it was the searing, tearing flame of hatred—hatred of Bran for his steadfastness, hatred of Abiris and of Carodoc and of the whole world he claimed had betrayed him. Evelake *could* have made the skillful, tortuous plan to steal the Arch Druid's jewel in such a way that the blame and the punishment would fall upon Bran.

But Evelake had been gone a day and a night from Carleon when the theft had taken place. Nor did it seem he could have bribed another to take the bead, for all who had been in the town that night were innocently accounted for from the time Peredur entered the room of the treasury to meet Bran until the time he was found the next morning asleep, and the bead gone. So much Abiris had said was certain and Carodoc felt relief that it was so. Evelake had been away from Carleon and, so, safe from the appearance of evil. He wondered idly what had taken him away when, by waiting another day, he could have gone along the forest track with Bran for company. No matter. At least his well-loved Evelake had not—could not—have committed the sacrilege.

But neither could Bran. For another reason, an unprovable reason to be sure, but a reason as true—even truer than Evelake's physical absence. Men like Bran did not do such things. It was not in their nature to do them. Somehow the facts that seemed so right must be wrong.

He stopped outside the ring of stones that enclosed the sacred fire. It burned clear and steady in the windless night. No. Night no longer. The first pale streak on the horizon already promised dawn and the first mist of morning was already rising in swirls that danced across the empty Ring of the Mighty Ones. The happy bonfires no longer streamed toward the sky. Their places were marked now by no more than smoldering embers. In the east the morning star was bright and green and, for a moment, Carodoc forgot the evil in the world and rested in its peace and silence.

He raised his arms to the eastern sky and prayed to Beli for guidance and help for Bran, feeling the weariness of the night and the stiff ache in his old wound. He moved away from the circle and went toward the mounds of earth thrown up so long ago by unknown hands for an unknown purpose.

He found Ysobel soon after, asleep in the mist at the foot of one of the mounds. He stood looking at her face and saw it strained and unhappy even in her sleeping.

As if her closed eyes sensed a presence, she moved restlessly and whimpered like a child in a bad dream. He hated to rouse her, to bring her out of whatever half oblivion she had found, back to a waking and sharp memory of Bran's clear and present danger. But he knew he must break the spell of her dreams. Abiris must be told she was found. So much could be done to lighten the old man's suffering. Somehow, she must be brought to make her own peace with their father. They must begin at once to look for some loose thread that would unravel the skein of lies and half truths tangled about Bran.

He leaned down to her and very gently smoothed the misty hair back from her forehead. She came at once awake and into an immediate awareness of the day and night just past. Her haunted face was so empty of any shadow of her quick laughter, so full of sorrow and pain, Carodoc could not speak his pity.

She released herself from the cocoon of the wolfskin and got to her feet and picked up the covering and folded it neatly, performing the motions mechanically. She did not put up a hand to arrange the tangled hair that fell wildly loose about her shoulders and this, too, was a pain to Carodoc, knowing her usual care for her person.

She looked at him almost hostilely and asked, as if she doubted his intentions, "Have you come to help, Carodoc?"

The look and the doubt in her voice sparked anger in him and he would have turned his back upon her distrust except that her eyes pleaded for his help and turned the spark quickly cold and he answered simply, "Yes."

"Let us go then to the horses and be on our way, for the truth is not here." She started toward the trackway that would take them most shortly back.

He stopped her. "Gently, little sister; we cannot ride off into this new day without thought or plan. Food at least we shall need for a journey of many days."

"Food! I vow before you, Carodoc, I will not taste food until Bran is free again."

He made himself speak sternly against the love and pity in his heart. "Ysobel! You speak as a witless child. How do you think to free Bran unless you keep your mind clear and your body strong? This will not be done in a day or yet in a week. I say to you we will both need all our wits and all our strength to do what must be done. This is no time for foolish vows. If we fail in our intent we will both sit in the ashes and take nor food nor drink. Now we have work to do."

She did not answer and started again toward the trackway. He thought she was shut away in the prison of her own misery. He knew he must, somehow, break through it if they were to help Bran. She was no good to anyone so. He spoke to her back. "Arrange your hair, Ysobel. You cannot come to our father, Abiris, like a—like a common drab."

She whirled about and her face came alive with anger and he thought it is good. At least she is no longer walking in a dream.

133

"Abiris! I will never come to him. From this day forth he is no more father to me."

He was shocked and a little frightened by her outburst. He took two long steps and came beside her and caught her shoulder roughly. "Do you know what you are saying, girl?"

She looked at him levelly and answered, "Abiris is unjust and cruel. He has betrayed us all. He would offer Bran as a sacrifice to Beli because there are no evildoers in our tribe and Abiris the Druid would not come empty-handed to his god at midsummer."

He shook her. Shook her hard until he could see dizziness in her eyes. "Be quiet!" he ordered, and stopped the shaking but held her still that she would not run from him. "You must not say such things. They are not true. You know they are not true. Have you not seen the horror and pain—yes, and the feeling of betrayal—that have made our father old in a single day? Or are you too wrapped in your own sorrow to spare a thought for him? He has loved Bran as his own son. He would gladly give his own life to believe Bran free of evil."

He felt her wince under his powerful grip. He was hurting her and he did not care. Her wanton talk of cruelty and sacrifices put her outside his pity. He had for her now only scorn and anger.

She was past caring, but she wanted to return hurt for hurt. "So," she said deliberately, "you have *not* come to help but to spy into my mind and to berate me for saying what is plain for all to see. I need your help. Beli knows I need it. But since you, too, believe Bran evil, I stand alone. Very well. Alone I will find the truth and fling it before Abiris and the Arch Druid at midsummer at the Henge."

The sun broke over the downs and stained the white mists rose and gold before they began to evaporate as if they had never been. He took his hand from her shoulder and put his arm about her. His anger was spent. He wanted only to find a way to make her see the need for calm and clear thought. "Ysobel, Ysobel. Did I not tell you I came to help? Have I ever spoken falsely to you? Anger and harsh words will not free Bran from the burden of these lies. He is my brother in all but blood and I love and trust him as I do not any other man. But this is not enough. It is not enough to *believe* him guiltless. It will need patient searching and long, clear thinking to find proof of his innocence, for nothing short of proof will free him now, and this you must know."

She held herself stiffly a moment longer; then her face crumpled and her body shuddered with sobs. He stood with her quietly until she could speak again. "Oh, Carodoc, I am so frightened and so miserable and so—so hopeless."

"Yes." He put into the one word all he could of comfort, knowing that, as yet, there was nothing more he could do.

"What will I do? What will I do?"

"We will seek," he told her; "seek through all of Britain, if need be; knock at every door, until somewhere we find the truth to free him."

If you seek, you will find. If you knock, the door will open.

Someone had said those words to her once. She could not now remember who or when. But the words brought her the first comfort she'd known since Bran had walked away from her between the men of the guard.

Carodoc saw that something had brought her a little courage. He said steadily, "First we must go to Abiris. You judge him too harshly, Ysobel. He, too, is broken with sorrow. And his sorrow is deeper than yours, for he does truly believe Bran a thief. Who are we to judge him, my sister, not having his heart and mind within us? Will you come and make your peace with him?"

She hesitated. She was listening again to ghost words from another time and another place she could not quite remember.

Do not judge another unless you are willing to be judged with the same judgment.

Carodoc was right. She could not know the ways of her father's heart. She had no right to judge him. "I will go and I will make peace," she said.

"Come then." He took her hand and led her to the trackway. They did not talk, each searching his mind for some starting point for the freeing of Bran, until they could see the pavilion and smell the cooking fires where Anya was preparing the morning meal. Ysobel said, then, what was in her mind. "If only Ganhelon had not sent to bid Evelake leave Carleon and take his hunting hounds to Brittany, there might be hope. I am sorry, Carodoc, but Evelake could——"

"*What did you say, Ysobel?*" Carodoc had stopped in the trackway and the words came sharp as pelting rain.

She thought, I've angered him suggesting his precious Evelake would steal. She could not care now. "Evelake would not keep his hands from theft, Carodoc. He was in Carleon until the night before the jewel disappeared. Had he but stayed, Bran would not be the only one to be suspected."

Carodoc made an impatient gesture. "Yes," he agreed, "that I know." She wondered that he did not rush to Evelake's defense. "What was it you said about hunting hounds and Ganhelon?"

"What does it matter? Come along now. We waste time when there is none to waste." She could not understand his willingness to stand here talking.

"It does matter, Ysobel. Tell me. Again. Slowly. All of it."

"There is little to tell. Evelake had promised Bran to come to the Arch Druid's house and see this Peredur. After sundown the night before, a message came for Bran. Ganhelon was sending hunting hounds to one in Brittany who would pay for them in silver coins. The villein who was to care for them upon the journey was, of a sudden, stricken with some sickness and Ganhelon would have Evelake cross the narrow water and deliver the hounds and receive the payment. Evelake, the message said, was leaving at once —as soon as he found food for himself and Annwyn. And that is all."

She wished she could read his thoughts. His head was dropped and she could not see his face. He touched his old wound questioningly, as she had seen him do before. She thought he had forgotten Bran, forgotten her, forgotten even where they were. She said, "Carodoc?" and he lifted his head and looked at her and his face was terrible to see. She caught her breath. "Carodoc. What is it? Are you ill?"

"Ill? No, Ysobel. Or only in my heart. Only for a hope and a dream destroyed forever, a faith betrayed."

"What is it, Carodoc? I do not understand these things you are saying? Have they anything to do with Bran?"

He spoke again, as if he spoke only to his own heart, as if he had not heard her questions. "He could have done it, then. I was glad he had not been there. I might still have had a chance to change him."

She pulled at his sleeve and raised her voice to bring his mind back to her. "Carodoc! Carodoc! Tell me."

He jerked at her touch and looked at her and moved his weak shoulder as if he were casting a heavy burden from it. "Evelake took no hunting hounds to Brittany, Ysobel," he said, and at her startled "what!" he raised his hand to silence her. "Hear me. On the very day before the theft I went to the house of Ganhelon to bring a new-made mirror for his wife. Ganhelon himself let me in and when he saw the mirror—a gay, pretty bauble scrolled and polished—he groaned aloud as a man sorely hurt. He bade me come in and gave me a horn of mead and begged pardon for his churlishness. He had, he said, forgot the mirror. Had he remembered in time he would surely have told me not to make it. For—and mark this well, Ysobel—he said he had planned to buy the mirror with silver coins he expected to receive from one in Brittany who liked his hunting hounds and had promised to send for them. But no word had come. The market for hounds had—it seemed—ceased on a sudden, or else his man had taken an illness, and the brutes still to be fed and cared for and never a denier of good Roman metal to be had for them. Ganhelon did not send to Evelake to beg his help in taking hunting hounds to Brittany, Ysobel."

She had felt the flame of hope rising in her as Carodoc talked. Evelake had not gone to Brittany. Therefore, she thought, Evelake—Evelake, not Bran—had stolen the Arch Druid's jewel. She tugged at Carodoc's hand. "Hurry. Hurry and tell our father, that he may have Bran set free at once."

Carodoc did not hurry. His eyes were pitying, but he spoke firmly. "Wait, little one. You go too fast. Evelake lied about the hounds. But do you not forget that there is none to say he did not leave Carleon for all that. His lie speaks of mischief, no doubt. But it does not clear Bran of suspicion. Not unless someone saw Evelake in Carleon on the night of the theft."

She could not believe what she heard. Surely he would not protect Evelake at Bran's expense. Or would he? "Would you then save Evelake though Bran died for it?" she asked, and saw his look of disdain and did not heed it. "Then I shall go to our father and tell him. Now."

He caught her arm and held her. "No," he shouted, and went on more quietly. "You have no proof. Abiris would not believe you without proof. Evelake's lie proves nothing in Bran's favor. Not yet. But hear me, Ysobel. I would not sacrifice the least of the villeins to save Evelake, if he is the thief, let alone leave *Bran,* my brother, to die in his stead. It may be true—I am afraid it is true that Evelake, whom I have cherished in my heart, has become a man possessed by the very spirit of evil. If this is so, I would not raise my smallest finger to preserve him. But his lie is not enough in itself to save Bran. It is, as yet, but a loose end in what has been a tight and endless ball of suspicion. It is, as yet, no more than a little mystery. But it may be a beginning."

"How then can we use it?" She felt shamed by her outburst at him. Someday she would tell him so. Now there was no time, for already they had lost two hours of the few they had before midsummer.

"This," he said crisply, glad to be planning some activity instead of thinking of his lost Evelake. "I will leave at once for Carleon. I will say I am come to buy gold and pearls and other things for my work at the forge. In truth I shall try to find one single person who saw Evelake in the town after he was supposed to be gone."

"Or Annwyn," she added.

"Or Annwyn," he agreed. "Meantime, do you go back to the village and keep your ears and your eyes alert for signs or whispers that may hint at the reason for Evelake's lie. Be careful, Ysobel. Keep your wits clear. Do not let your mind be confused with fear for Bran. Somehow, when I am in Carleon, I will get word to him that we are working for him. And I will come again as quickly as I can. Is it well?"

She thought it would have to be since there was nothing else they could do. She wished she could go to Carleon with him but knew he would go more quickly alone. She agreed, "It is well," and he said, "Come then. Let us go to Abiris. But say no word of this to him, Ysobel. Without proof he might—he might accuse us of preparing a false witness and forbid our plan. A small deceit now may prevent a great wrong later."

CHAPTER ELEVEN

Bran heard in silence the Arch Druid's command to take him as a prisoner to Carleon, there to wait out the time until midsummer, when all the tribes would send their criminals to be judged and punished at Beli's Henge. He was stunned and exhausted by the events of this weary, long day. Numbness descended upon his mind and made of it a blank and useless thing. During the journey back to Carleon he walked by day and slept by night, surrounded by his guards, in a half-conscious stupor.

The stupor broke when they brought him to a tall wicker cage set near the Arch Druid's house and opened the cage door and bade him enter, mocking him with coarse talk. He looked at them and at himself and saw himself for the first time in many days—saw the dirty, torn breeches and shirt they had substituted for his blue robe; saw his hands, chafed at the wrists by the rubbing of the leather thongs that bound them. He saw, too, the cage that would be his prison and his funeral pyre and he was filled with horror and fear. The guards waited, laughing, watching realization reach him. One of them nudged another and said, "Look at him now, Gwyth, and own you've lost your wager. See! The swine knows his doom right enough. Thought he could let Peredur suffer for his crime, did he? Bran the Brave indeed! Bran the Coward and Thief."

Fear and anger and frustration came together in Bran's mind and exploded and he whirled and hit out with his bound hands at the guard who had spoken and saw him fall and the rest of the men gaping with open mouths and unready. He started to smash a path to freedom through them.

Run. Run. Run. The words beat in his brain and his feet obeyed them. Two spearmen went down as he lowered his head and butted their stomachs like a he-goat gone mad. And two more. He heard their spears clatter on the cobbled street and thrust forward again. He was, he thought, almost clear. Sixty heartbeats more and he could turn a remembered corner and be, for a moment, safe even from the whistling arrows the bowmen would surely send after him so soon as they got back their wits.

He did not see the foot thrust forward to trip him. He fell heavily, hitting his forehead on the rough stones. He felt the blow and felt nothing more until he knew he was being thrust roughly through the cage door. He struggled then, forgetting his aching head, but his struggles were useless against the strong hands that held him now. They threw him to the floor of the cage and rammed the door shut and iron rang on iron as they shot home the heavy bolts.

He got to his knees and faced them through the tough interlacings of the wickerwork. The guard called Gwyth snatched a spear from a man beside him and started, holding the spear before him, toward the cage. Bran thought he is going to kill me and thought he did not care. Better die now quickly on a spear than later in the fires at the Henge.

Two of the others outside the cage seized Gwyth and

held him. Someone said, "Have you lost your wits, Gwyth? He is god-dedicated now and, besides, he's safe enough. You well know it is you will suffer for it if he comes marked in his body to the sacrifice."

Gwyth did not take his eyes from Bran's face. They were little eyes, half lost in ridges of flesh and red with hatred. Gwyth said, "He hit me, the son of evil," and tried to break away from his fellows.

"Do you go and get the rods then. They'll bring him pain enough and their marks will be gone by midsummer."

Gwyth smiled—a slow, cruel smile that caused his eyes to disappear completely in their fat ridges—and nodded and left and the others came close to the cage and watched. Bran tried to get to his feet and fell forward on his face again. The watching men rocked with laughter and Bran felt sickness in him as he realized his loneliness and helplessness.

He shouted at them, "Take me out of here. Take me to the Arch Druid. I have done no evil. *No evil*, I tell you."

They jeered at him, imitating his desperation. "Take me to the Arch Druid. I have done no evil."

Bran beat his hands on the floor of the cage and tried to speak reasonably. "Which of you is captain of this guard?"

A tall, brawny man said, "I am," and would have gone on had not Bran interrupted quickly. "Do you give me at least a piece of birchbark and a knife that I may write out my innocence."

The captain stepped forward and motioned the guards back a little until he stood alone and clear before the cage. "Quiet!" he ordered to still the chattering and laughter of his men and when they were silent he spat in Bran's face. "*That* I will give you, warlock and murderer. That and no more. I was friend to Peredur, do you hear? Friend and companion to the finest soldier that ever stood a guard. You,

son of all evil, you drugged him and stole the sacred jewel
and caused him to be driven forth from this place. Peredur
went to the great King Cymbeline and took service with
him and died fighting his battles. You killed Peredur. You
killed my friend. Were it not forbidden, I would, with my
own hands, tear your loathsome heart from your evil body."

Peredur dead! It could not be. Bran thought, this man
is trying to trick me. He looked at the faces peering at him
and saw the grim, set expressions, saw them hating and loathing him, and knew what the captain said of Peredur's death
was true and bowed his head, feeling his own hot tears wash
the spittle from his face.

He did not know that Gwyth had returned until he felt
himself dragged from the cage again and felt his back muscles jerk under lashings that seared him with pain. He shut
his teeth over his lips and endured the lashes, summoning
his pride to keep from crying out before his tormentors.

Gwyth left off at last and they threw Bran again into
his prison and the guards withdrew. He could hear them
laughing and talking of their families and the mead they
would drink and the food they would eat with lighter hearts
because that son of evil was safely brought to his prison.
Only Gwyth did not go. He took his station to one side
of the cage and watched Bran with a look full of malice and
hating. Bran sat with his head bent on his knees, his eyes
closed against the presence of Gwyth, and tried to prepare
his soul for the long waiting till midsummer.

The following days crawled as slowly as snakes that had
just shed their skins at winter's end. His thoughts whirled
about and about and came always back to a vision of himself
in the loathsome cage, burning in the fires of the Henge
under the full moon of midsummer. They brought him food,
good and plentiful. The first time he turned away from it

and Gwyth and another held him and forced the food into his mouth and held his mouth shut until he swallowed the thick pottage, because he must. After that, he ate what was brought rather than suffer the indignity of their force. He asked one of them, a man more kindly than the rest, why they cared whether he ate or not and the man said he must not be taken scrawny and lean to the sacrifice. They must fatten me, Bran thought bitterly, even as they fatten the white bullocks for the sacred knife.

They took him each day to the War Field outside the town and set up a mark and gave him a great bow and a single arrow. He must, they said, keep his body lithe and his muscles strong for the god. The first day he refused to shoot as he had refused to eat, but Gwyth threatened him with the slender rods and, to save himself the sharp pains, he shot and ran to fetch the arrow and shot again and again and again. For all the rest of the slow hours he cowered in his cage and his mind raced from terror to despair and back again and he knew himself deserted by everyone, even Evelake and Carodoc, his friends—even Ysobel, his beloved. He cursed them all and cursed himself and shivered with fear of Gwyth and the cruel rods and did not see the curious folk who came to stare at him, always keeping a safe distance away, fearing his witchcraft.

It was thus, from a distance, as part of the gaping crowd, that Carodoc saw him.

Carodoc had come to Carleon no more than a few hours after Bran had been thrown into the cage, and he had found lodgings in the house of the smith. Each day he had gone to the shops and pretended he could not find just what he sought and must return again and yet again. He kept his ears open for talk of the theft and, feigning ignorance, asked his careful questions, seeking always to find a thin place for doubt in the web of evidence against Bran.

On the second day of his stay in Carleon he came upon Shawn, the smith's boy, a frail lad with a withered arm, ringed about with older, stronger boys taunting his weakness and threatening to beat him. Shawn had courage and intelligence. He stood among them, glaring defiance, his good arm taut to defend himself. Carodoc was filled with quick anger. He caught one of the tormentors by the shoulder and spun him about and hit him hard and clean upon the point of his chin and knocked him down. The others, taken by surprise, turned their attention from the smith's boy and Carodoc had time to call out, "Run, Shawn, run," thinking he could not hold the pack long. They turned upon him, yelling. He fought them skillfully, and when he had laid two more of them low the rest ran, for they were bullies who would not stand to a real fight even with such odds on their side.

It was only then, when Carodoc stooped to help his first victim to his feet and give him a tongue lashing, that he saw Shawn had not run but stood beside him, one eye already closing from a buffet he had caught, grinning at his benefactor.

"Why didn't you run, Shawn?"

"And leave you to fight my battle alone? I'd not do that, Car-doc. I've one good arm and my teeth are fair sharp and I can kick right truly. They're nothing but—but low fellows. I could likely have licked the lot of them."

Carodoc smiled at the boy's boasting. "I'm sure you could, Shawn," he agreed solemnly and the boy wiped his nose on his sleeve and said, "I thank you, Car-doc, for all that."

"Come then. Let us go together to your mother, Shawn.

She will poultice your eye with mistletoe and I will tell her you were not at fault."

After that, Shawn dogged his footsteps, and he was glad, for the boy knew all the gossip of the town and talked readily and openly of the stolen jewel. He talked, too, half fearfully, half excitedly, of Bran the Warlock, prisoner in the cage.

Carodoc kept away from Bran for many days. He did not want the people of the town to guess his real reason for being in Carleon. Feeling against the warlock and thief was high and Carodoc thought he would get no answers to his question if it were known he sought to help the prisoner. He let six nights go by before he joined the gapers and saw his friend huddled, dirty and unkempt, on the cage floor. The sight galled him and added to his sense of failure. He turned out of the crowd, disgusted at their sordid curiosity, sick with pity for Bran the Brave, who had been brought so low.

Despair closed in upon him. Wherever he questioned, he received the same answers—hopeless answers for him and for Bran. No one had seen Evelake and Annwyn in Carleon on the day or the night of the theft. Many swore to their departure, equipped as for a long journey. Many testified they had left the city at dusk, going eastward at a fast pace, on the night before the thieving. They were all sure Evelake had gone. They were all ready to swear he could not have returned unseen. Every man in Carleon was alert that night because they feared the Belgae. Peredur himself, upon an alarm being raised at some strange movement near the Arch Druid's house, had searched the whole town and found only a mongrel dog.

Yet, Carodoc thought as he walked back to the smith's house with Shawn chattering beside him, yet Evelake *had* lied when he said he was going to Brittany. There was but one other thing he could do. He could see the scar-faced man who had been in the treasury when Bran left. But that man had gone on the day of the Beltane upon a journey for the Arch Druid. He should return, Shawn had said, any day.

Carodoc wondered whether there was any sense in waiting out the time. He was worried for Ysobel. She would be each day expecting his return and the waiting would be hard for her. Had she seen Evelake or heard anything of him? He had best leave Carleon, he decided, on the morrow, and yet —and yet, if he left without talking to the scar-faced man, how could he ever be sure he had done everything possible for Bran? He wished he could be given a sign.

Shawn pulled at his breeches and Carodoc looked down at the boy and smiled a little. "What are you thinking, Car-doc? Your face is black as my father's forge."

Carodoc thought he must remember to school his face in Shawn's presence. He laughed a little. "What man can see his own face, Shawn? I was but thinking I must be soon away from here, for my own forge waits."

"Do not go yet, Car-doc. Stay yet a little longer. I—I will miss you."

Carodoc thought, why not? Could such a thing as a small boy's plea be the sign he wanted? He ran his hand through Shawn's yellow curls and decided it could be. "Very well, Shawn. I will stay a little longer and we will go each day to the venders and you shall help me choose what I need and if your father will lend me his forge I will make a pin for your mantle."

"Hola! Hola! Hola! I would like that Car-doc. Will you make me a wolf pin? I will be strong like a wolf when I am older."

"Yes, Shawn. I will fashion your pin in the shape of a

148

wolf and I will set a charm upon it and it will keep you safe from all evil."

"Can you really make a charm, Car-doc?" Shawn's eyes were wide with wonder.

Carodoc began to say there were no charms and changed his mind, thinking there would be time enough for Shawn to lose his sense of wonder. The boy would need all the help he could get, and who knew but the very belief in a charm would hold a power for strength. "Do you not know, Shawn, that I am of the ancient people?"

"Ah-h-h. I had forgot, Car-doc," Shawn said, and ran ahead to tell his mother of the wolf pin.

Making the pin gave Carodoc the excuse he needed to wait out the days until Scarface would return. He worked slowly, taking deliberate and unnecessary time. Each day he went to one of the venders and bought gold or pearls, amber or colors, which he would use later in his own forge.

Early on the morning of the fifth day he put the final touch to the gold pin, cunningly worked into the form of a grinning wolf's mask, and went to the door to call Shawn. He opened his mouth to shout and closed it again as he saw a man with a scarred face and travel-stained clothes striding down the cobbled street. Today, then, would be the end of his stay in Carleon. He would see the man later and he would know, no matter what the end of their talk, he had done all he could. He watched Scarface until he turned in at the door of a house a little distance away, and sighed and called Shawn.

The boy came running and shouted with delight when he saw the pin completed. He tried to thank Carodoc and could find no words, but the shining in his eyes was thanks enough. Carodoc pinned the mask on his shirt, since in the hot day the lad needed no mantle, and when Shawn ran to show the pin to his mother Carodoc followed after him.

When they had eaten the midday meal Shawn went with Carodoc to the smith's forge and watched while Carodoc cleaned and packed his own fine tools. The boy's eyes were sad and Carodoc tried to comfort him. "I will come back again, Shawn. Do not grieve for my going."

Shawn tried to smile. "I cannot help it, Car-doc. I will truly miss you. I wish—I wish there were a thing I could do for you before you go."

"There is, Shawn, if you are stout of heart."

"*What*, Car-doc? Tell me what it is. I will not be afraid. I promise."

"Will you, then, carry me a message to the prisoner in the cage?"

"To the—the *warlock?*"

"To Bran the Brave, Shawn. He is no warlock, but my friend and unjustly accused. Do you think you could come near him without the guard seeing you?"

"Surely." The boy looked his scorn at such a question. Any boy could do as much. Then his face lengthened. "But, Car-doc, I dare not. He could—he could *witch* me."

Carodoc sighed. He couldn't expect young Shawn to believe Bran's innocence, not with the evidence of his own eyes that the man was caged as only murderers and warlocks were. He said softly, "You promised you would not be afraid, Shawn."

Shawn's face was screwed tight in misery. He fingered his new pin and tried to find courage to do as Carodoc asked him. He wanted to, but—a warlock!

Carodoc touched the pin. "Did I not tell you I would put upon the pin a charm to keep you from evil?"

Shawn looked at him and looked at the wolf mask and his face cleared. "Did you truly do so, Car-doc?"

Carodoc nodded, thinking the lie justified, since no harm would come to the boy through Bran.

"Well, I will go then. But, to be sure, I'll get some beans from my mother. Beans are good against witch spells and I can spit right truly."

Bran became aware of a small urchin when something hit his shoulder with so sharp a sting it jerked him from his daze of misery. He raised his head and glared at the guard but the man, not Gwyth, was leaning, half asleep, on his spear. There was no one about and Bran noticed that it was early morning and guessed the town was not yet awake. Another sharp sting brought his head away from the guard and he saw the boy, his first and little fingers stretched against evil, his lips compressed in the act of spitting. Bran saw the small pellet as it came toward him and moved his shoulders even as he knew the pellet was a bean, and thought drearily that if he were in truth a warlock he would use his spells to free himself from these hateful bonds. He started to make an ugly face at the boy, wanting to frighten away this minor irritation, and stopped himself. He wondered, his mind moving slowly, why the boy was here at this hour, alone and close to the cage. He raised a bound hand and beckoned and the boy came a step nearer and whispered, "There is a man yonder." He pointed over his shoulder and Bran, straining his eyes in the early light, could make out in the distance the small, dark shape of a man. "His name's Car-doc," Shawn whispered, and saw a change in the warlock's face. "Says tell you do not lose hope. Says somewhat else—somewhat of a lady as is waiting, but I have forgotten."

The guard stirred and awoke and raised his head, listening, and Shawn dropped to his belly and crawled quickly away, hidden from the guard by the cage. Bran shifted his cramped legs and raised his head and for the first time in many days smelled the cool, clean air redolent in the early morning of pine and cedar from the forest. I am not forgotten, he thought. Carodoc and Ysobel, they will find the truth and they will free me and his blood surged in his veins with the new hope that had come to him in the new day.

CHAPTER TWELVE

THE time that followed the Beltane tried Ysobel's patience. She had expected Carodoc's return within ten nights, but he did not come so soon. The ten nights passed and nine more and she tried to endure the waiting resolutely, tried not to think of Bran. Her face ached each day from holding it proud and smiling for all to see, but at night fear for Bran came out from hiding and companioned her wakefulness. She lost weight and color and walked pale as a moon spirit along the village lanes.

If, she thought, if only she had been able to find some crumb of the truth they sought to hoard against Carodoc's return. But there was nothing. Her ears and her eyes burned with strain. She saw nothing except the lake reeds in their fresh summer green; heard nothing but the cries of water-fowl, raucous and lonely, and the open talk of Bran's witch-craft. She collected the tales of his witchings as she heard them—a cow gone suddenly dry, a young boy stricken dumb and motionless, a field of corn that would not come to ear. These rumors she nicked out carefully upon bark and sent by a villein to Abiris to investigate. There was a little comfort in it, but only a little, for she could find no hint that might clear Bran of the charge of theft.

Nor was there any sign of Evelake. He had vanished as if he had never been, and Annwyn, the Swineherd, had vanished with him. Hiding her distress and her distaste of anything to do with Evelake, she went to Ganhelon's house. She took, as excuse, a gift of dressed fowl and bore the aimless, endless chatter of Evelake's mother, hoping to hear of his whereabouts. She had as well stayed home. Ganhelon and his wife could not or would not say where their son was. He had gone fishing perhaps. Or hunting. Or to see the great King Cymbeline. Or simply about his own business. He was no longer a child to seek permission for his goings and his comings. He came when he willed and went when he willed and where.

She could do nothing more. Nothing but wait for Carodoc and blow upon the dwindling flame of her hope to keep it alive.

When he came, at last, tired and discouraged, the flame died and she could not revive it. He told her of his failure in Carleon, told her how he had lingered to see the scar-faced guard, hoping that in his story he might find some small hope. The waiting had been useless. Scarface, like all the other soldiers of the Arch Druid's guard, hated Bran because they believed he had planned that Peredur should bear the blame for the theft.

"Was there then nothing?" she asked. "*Nothing*, in all the troubled time after the jewel vanished, out of the ordinary?"

"Yes. There was one thing, but it holds no help for us or Bran. One of the Arch Druid's villeins, a kin-shattered man who had come from no one knows where—a surly, quarrelsome brute of a man named Tostig—has not been seen in Carleon since a week after the theft."

Her face lighted with excitement. "But surely, Carodoc,

surely he could have been the thief. Has there been no search——"

Carodoc put his hand upon her arm to stop her. "Hear me out, my sister. The man Tostig was indeed suspect. He was a kitchen villein in the Arch Druid's house and he had the run of the place. He could, perhaps, have drugged Peredur's cup. But none could show how he could come by any drug, and he could not have taken the jewel, for he was able to bring witnesses to say he had not left the common room where all the villeins sleep during the whole night. He and four trustworthy men had played at dice from shortly after dusk until near dawn. No one in the town was surprised when this Tostig left. He had often threatened to go away. His going was good riddance. Nothing more."

She asked him, then, about Bran, and he replied briefly. He had seen him, but only from a distance. He had found a lad willing to take a message to the prisoner and had sent a careful word to let Bran know he was not deserted. More he would not tell her. She tried to get past the guard he had set upon his words, but he put her pleadings aside and she knew at last, or thought she knew, that Bran was being subjected to indignities, even cruelties, Carodoc could not bring himself to describe, and her heart was cold and hard within her.

Time was their enemy. There were now less than thirty nights before midsummer. Twenty-seven nights before the festival in Beli's Great Circle at the Henge, that had been built, some said, by giants when the world was young and would endure until time stopped. Twenty-seven nights, and no matter how they two beat at their brains, they could think of nothing more to do.

Unless they could find Evelake—find him and force him to admit guilt—Bran would die. Carodoc sent villeins to search—for Annwyn, since he did not want to make it clear he suspected Evelake. The swineherd's hut was empty, his fire dead, and there was no sign of him in the forest. After that there was nothing. Nothing but unfulfilled waiting and the passing of days that could not be held back.

On the seventh day of the new month, fourteen days before midsummer night, Ysobel stood before her loom listlessly passing the shuttle back and forth, weaving plain dun cloth because she had no spirit for intricate patterns in colors. The long shadows of the afternoon had crept closer while she worked, until now they had shrouded the loom and she could not see the warp. She left the shuttle caught midway and turned away. The house was heavy and hot. The smoke from the smoldering hearth fire hung thick and gray and low. She went to the door, hoping that the outside air would refresh her, and saw the western sky piled high with dark, massed clouds and the lake water dull and brooding under them. Behind her, Anya was moving and grumbling to one of the other villeins.

Carodoc came around the corner of the house. She started to call out to him and held her call when she saw his finger on his lips commanding silence. They could no longer talk openly together about Bran because the villagers guessed they were helping him and resented it. She could see that he was excited and her heart lifted a little. He looked about him stealthily and she followed his looking. There was no one in the brooding heat of the lanes, no one upon the brooding lake. He beckoned her and, after a quick glance inside the house to be sure she was not watched, she joined him and they went quietly to the landing and untied Carodoc's boat and got into it and he steered the dugout under the village palisade until it was hidden by a screen of willows and tied it. He inched his way toward her until he could kneel beside her in the flat bottom.

"What is it, Carodoc? Have you found Evelake?"

He shook his head. "No, though for the past two nights from dusk to dawn I have watched Ganhelon's house."

"Why? Have you reason to think . . ."

"No. No reason. Just a hope that Evelake would come, or send Annwyn, for food or silver coins. Neither came, but I could not seem to stay away. Today I could not rest, though I knew there'd be no coming in daylight if Evelake has—anything—to hide. I slept a little, or tried to, and went back to watch."

Excitement tickled her scalp and she broke in on his story. "What? What did you see?"

"Something was going on in Ganhelon's house. There were a stirring and a bustling beyond the ordinary. I kept my watch, and when the sun had passed the noonstead, Ganhelon and his wife and all their house villeins came out. The villeins carried food and pavilions, saddles and bridles, and all things needed for a journey of some nights."

Disappointment pressed in on her. So Ganhelon and his wife were going upon a journey. What help was that to Bran? "Is that all?" she asked in a thin flat voice, and he made an impatient gesture. "I came nearer until I could hear the talk between Ganhelon and his wife. He bade her cease her fretting. They were only going a little to the east to bide a while with her kin before the midsummer festival. Everything needful had been done. Then, Ysobel, then she threw her hands over her head and squealed like a young pig and said, 'The chest, Ganhelon. Evelake's little chest! Did you remember it?' and he gave her such a look of disgust and anger and said, 'Still your chattering tongue, woman! Would you tell Evelake's secrets to the whole village?' and she said, more quietly but loud enough for me to hear, 'But have you got it Ganhelon?' "

Carodoc stopped a moment for breath and Ysobel urged him on. "Yes. Go on. Go on, Carodoc."

"Ganhelon looked all about him before he answered and it was well I had taken care to flatten myself close against the side of the house. Ganhelon said, "The chest is well hidden here, woman, for it was this Evelake bade me do. It is safe. Do you fear not. Safe in a place the boy knows of and can find when he has a mind to.' They went away then, toward the landing place, and I followed them and saw them cross to the eastern shore."

"Evelake's little chest," Ysobel said slowly. "Evelake's little chest. Do you suppose, Carodoc, he would have dared hide the Arch Druid's jewel here in his own house?"

"It does not seem likely. And yet . . . and yet . . . I do not know what he might do, thinking himself safe. I know only that somehow we must see for ourselves what is hidden."

"How? How can we? I doubt Ganhelon has gone on a journey leaving his house unguarded."

"No. But guards do often grow careless when the night is far spent. Tonight, I think, we will try to get into Ganhelon's house and find the chest and look into it."

"Tonight! Yes, it had best be this night. Carodoc, do you suppose . . ."

"Supposing will get us nowhere, Ysobel. It is but a waste of time. Do you go now and eat and rest. Sleep if you can. When the water clock marks midnight I will come for you and we will go together to the house of Ganhelon and you will watch while I search out what is hidden."

"You should eat, too, Carodoc."

"I have a packet of honey cakes here." He touched a fold

of his tunic. "And I had best keep away from you until the villeins are deep asleep. We want no breath of suspicion running ahead of us."

He pulled the boat back to the landing and she left him and went to her house. She had not thought to sleep, but at the midnight hour Carodoc had to shake her, a hand ready to cover any startled outcry she might make. She followed him as silent as a cloud around the sleeping villeins and through the door he had left open and waited while he eased it closed, inch by quiet inch, lest there be a squeak from the hinges. The clouds that had shadowed the sunset now covered the whole sky, hiding the friendly stars. There was no light to mark the outlines of houses in the sleeping village, no sound of living thing in all the empty world.

She waited, hardly breathing, until Carodoc took her hand. She could see his eyes gleaming out of the blackness and was thankful for that legacy from their mother's race that enabled him to see as well by night as by day. She wondered, as they walked the deserted lanes, how it came about that he had in him so much of the dark, old tribes of the west and she had so little. Beli's ways were strange. She wished, with a feeling of having lost a thing of great value, that she could still think Beli's ways were also good. How could she when the god had left Bran, who served him well, to suffer for a crime he had surely not committed? How could a god whose ways were good permit such evil to exist in the world? She found her thoughts turning again to the god of Joshua ben Joseph who was a father to his people and wanted from them only love and obedience. She remembered her sense of guilt when last she'd thought of these things, her relief that Abiris could not know her secret mind, and she wondered why she had felt so. She no longer cared what Abiris might think. She had now only scorn for all the

Druids, who were willing to let Bran bear the blame they could not place elsewhere.

Carodoc pulled at her hand to stop her and pointed ahead, where light winked clear and bright through the darkness. A star, she thought, and looked at the sky, expecting to see the clouds broken, and found them black and threatening as before. She shook herself to free her mind of her own wandering thoughts and the spell of the night.

Carodoc pulled at her again and moved away from the houses toward the palisade. She followed him until they were clear of anyone who might be alert to hear their whispering.

"The light," she breathed. "It is in Ganhelon's house, Carodoc. You must have been wrong about their journeying. We'd best go back."

"No, Ysobel. I tell you Ganhelon and all his household are gone. The house was dark and empty less than an hour ago and the guard huddled asleep in his cloak as I guessed he would be. I have been watching."

"But, Carodoc, *someone* is there. Rushlights do not kindle themselves. How can you search out the chest?"

"Ysobel!" He sounded exasperated. "Wake up, girl. Do you not see? It *must* be Evelake or Annwyn come sneaking back for the chest. This may be the very chance we've waited. Now hear me. Make no sound. Hold fast to my sleeve, and when I jerk my arm downwards, do you stoop quickly and on no account speak."

She clutched his sleeve and he led her roundabout back to Ganhelon's until they could see the open door and the light coming through it. He jerked his arm downward and she crouched as he was crouching and crept forward as he was creeping until they could see through the door. They were beyond the light line, well hidden by the dark. The house within seemed bright by contrast, though there was only one rushlight and the ever-burning fire to show them Evelake on the hearth bench, bent forward, intent upon something hidden in his hands, and Annwyn, flattened against the pine bole that reached toward the roof.

Neither Evelake nor Annwyn moved for the space of sixty heartbeats. Then Evelake turned toward Annwyn, holding out his hands, and the light was caught and split into a blaze of golden splinters by the sunburst that surrounded the Arch Druid's V-shaped bead.

Ysobel, forgetting everything except the glory in Evelake's hands, would have cried out had not Carodoc covered her mouth, none too gently, with one hand. Holding her silent, he eased her away from the lighted house, and that which was within it, into the deeper shadows.

When they were perhaps ten paces from the house she began to struggle silently against his hand and he released her, knowing she had her sense again. He got to his feet and helped her up and they went to the safety of the palisade.

"You saw?" he whispered, and she said, "Let us go at once to Abiris. He must believe what his own eyes see."

"Gently, Ysobel," he warned her. "Let us think before we act. I doubt those two in Ganhelon's house will stay for us to send for Abiris."

"Then we must go ourselves to our father and tell him what we have seen. He will believe us. He must."

"Yes," Carodoc said, but she heard uncertainty in his agreement. "Yes, Abiris would, I think, believe us. But I do not trust Evelake. He is crafty as a boar cornered by huntsmen."

There was nothing, he thought with wonder and sadness, nothing left of his old love for the man whose life he had saved. He could almost hate Evelake. He did hate the evil in him. It was clear now, as clear as if he had seen it with his own eyes, that Evelake had taken the chevron bead. But there was still no witness to say he or Annwyn had been in Carleon on the night of the theft. Carodoc shivered in the hot, still air. Was Evelake a warlock? Some said a true witch had the power to make himself invisible.

Ysobel asked, "What else can we do, Carodoc? Surely if Abiris believes we saw Evelake with the bead he must believe him the thief."

"Put yourself, remembering his cunning, in Evelake's place, my sister. What would you do if you were Evelake and Abiris found you in possession of the stolen jewel?"

She thought about it, trying to imagine herself inside Evelake's mind. "I would," she said slowly, thinking it out, "I would, likely, deny the theft. So long as—so long as none could prove me in Carleon, I would—I would think myself fair safe."

"Yes," he agreed. "I think Evelake would do so. And I think he would go further. I think he would try to fasten the blame more tightly to Bran's back."

Her own thoughts were running ahead of him and she felt him watching her, though the night held his face from her.

"What else are you thinking, Ysobel?" he asked.

"I'm thinking what Evelake might think. He hates Bran, though I know not why. I believe he has planned all this to bring death to Bran." She spoke as if she were in a trance and he did not interrupt her. "If he is caught now with the bead he will take his strong oath as a free man that Bran had given him the bead for safekeeping."

Carodoc said, "I am sure you are right. Evelake could well say he agreed to help Bran for their sworn friendship, that he thought Bran had some secret reason for hiding the jewel—some good and honest reason, that, in his own time, he would explain. And so, knowing in truth that Bran had never taken the bead, Evelake would provide the final proof of Bran's guilt—the jewel itself."

She nodded in the dark. "He means to make certain Bran will die, Carodoc. How can we stop him?"

"I have been thinking, Ysobel, and I have a plan. The light still shines in Ganhelon's house, but I think it will not shine much longer. The day is not far off. Already the dawn breeze is rising. I think Evelake and Annwyn will soon leave the house and go to the place where they are hiding. I will follow them and discover their secret place and come to you tomorrow and together we will find a way to trap them."

"You will need a boat and they may not go by the landing stage but through some gap they have made in the palisade."

"I think you are right, but I shall need no boat. A boat, no matter how carefully oared, would be heard upon the water. I shall slip into the lake behind them and thank the good man who taught me long ago to swim as well as the very fish."

"Yes. I had forgotten. You'd best go quickly, and good fortune go with you, my brother."

He went away from her and, as his shadowy figure merged with the darker shadows, the light went out. She stayed where she was until she heard the little splash of a boat moving cautiously and, at once, because her ears were stretched for the further sound, a softer splash and knew that Carodoc was close behind the boat and would not lose Evelake and Annwyn until he had found their hiding place.

CHAPTER THIRTEEN

She found the hidden break in the palisade late on the following day and huddled beside it, taking, among the marsh reeds, what shelter she could from the drizzle of rain that threatened to become a steady downpour. The stormy dark came early down about her and she watched the dance of the marsh fires and heard the eerie, booming call of a bittern and looked for Carodoc and each moment grew colder and wetter and more miserable. Yet she did not see him, when he came at last pushing through the reeds behind her, nor hear him, so stealthily did he move.

"Is it you, Ysobel?" he whispered, and she jerked her head toward him, knowing his voice but unable to stay the trail of fear in her mind. She caught her breath sharply and put out her hand to him in welcome. "What did you find?" she asked.

He was wet and shivering. "We cannot talk here, my sister. Your clothes are soaked as mine are. You'd best go quickly and change them and meet me at the forge. We shall be secret enough there on such a night as this."

She hoped Anya would not be about to scold and harry her, and breathed more freely when she saw the house empty. No doubt the villeins had taken advantage of her absence to visit their friends in other houses and talk behind their hands of witches and warlocks. There were few in the village, tribesmen and villeins alike, who did not keep handy these days a bean to spit against a warlock—or a witch. She wondered when one of them would accuse her—or Carodoc—openly of witchcraft because it was known they believed Bran innocent.

The fire warmed her and stopped the shaking of her hands and she stripped off her clothes and dressed again quickly and hurried to the forge, the wolfskin from her bed wrapped about her to keep the warmth in and the rain out. She had caught up an earthen jug of mead and was glad she had done so, for Carodoc was shivering beside his forge fire and seemed unable to stop. After a moment he told her how he had stalked Evelake and Annwyn.

He had followed them easily enough, for they had taken no care to move quietly, thinking themselves alone in the breaking day. They had gone deeper and deeper into parts of the forest unknown to him and he had kept his distance, taking care to cut upon the trees secret signs that would mark the trail for him. After what he reckoned to be three hours, they had come out upon bare, clean downs and a little cave cunningly cut in the chalky soil and screened by a furze bush in full, golden blossom.

He had found a thick cedar copse and hidden himself within it and watched. He had seen Evelake come out with his great bow and a dozen heron-feathered arrows and go off into the forest again, obviously bent upon hunting game for their food. Annwyn did not show himself, and when, by early afternoon, Evelake had not returned, Carodoc had come away and back to her.

"What is next to do?" she asked him when he had finished—asked dispiritedly, for she saw no hope in what he had told her.

She thought he was as dispirited as she. "I could go again and keep a watch," he suggested, but she could see that he had no conviction that watching would help. She waited, and after a time he went on. "There is a mystery there, Ysobel. A mystery beyond the Arch Druid's bead, which is, indeed, no mystery, save in the manner of its taking."

"What mystery?"

"Annwyn. It is plain to see he fears Evelake, fears him and, I think, hates him. Yet Evelake goes forth boldly. I do not doubt he goes each day, for he could find no pleasure in the companionship of the swineherd. I do believe Annwyn could tell us all we need to know of the theft of the bead, yet it is plain Evelake does not fear he will run away. Why does he not? Is it not strange?"

She told him then, in spite of her promise of silence, how she had gone with Bran and seen Evelake driving the pin into the pain-free spot upon his leg, filling Annwyn with superstitious fear. "I think," she suggested, "I do think Annwyn believes Evelake to be the very Lord of Evil, who has put on the shape of a man. Such belief would come naturally to a poor creature like Annwyn. He would see no reason to run, since no man, he would think, could escape a god."

Carodoc's eyes were filled with disgust and pity. "Poor witless creature. There must be a way to free him. There must be. . . ."

He was still, suddenly, and the stillness was heavy with his thoughts. When he spoke again, his tiredness was lost in a new excitement.

"Annwyn, Ysobel! You are right. Annwyn could be the answer to all our need. What Evelake did, Annwyn saw. If he could be freed from his fear of Evelake, if I could reassure him, make him see that Evelake is no god but an ill-made man . . ." He struck his hands together. "I will go tomorrow and wait to find Annwyn alone and talk to him as a friend. He has, I think, no fear of me."

"I will go with you," she said, and when he would have denied her, she stopped him. "No, Carodoc. Hear me. I cannot sit here, doing nothing, alone, feared and distrusted by all in the village, thinking always of Bran and fearing for him, imagining horrors. Not one day more. Besides, it may be, since I am a woman and less—less fearsome, I may succeed with Annwyn where you might fail. You need not fear to take me. I shall not delay you, nor lag behind with weariness, nor complain, nor make undue noise."

He smiled at her then, and she thought she'd not seen his smile since the Beltane, and the sight of it lifted her heart. "Do you come then, for I see your mind is woman-fixed to go—and, in truth, I will be glad of your company. Now, let us get to the house, for I am hungry, having eaten nothing but roots and herbs these many hours. Let us eat and sleep and be ready to leave when the sun rises on the morrow."

They came next morning to the high downs in a day still overcast, though the rain had stopped. Carodoc guided her to the cedar copse and pointed out the golden bush that kept the cave mouth secret. They were scarcely hidden when Annwyn came from behind the bush, his twisted legs moving in an awkward, shuffling waddle that reminded Ysobel of the great blue herons as they fished among the reeds. He carried a bone, and when he had looked aimlessly about him, he sat with his back against the hillside and gnawed at the bone before he flung it away and began to sing—if the weird chanting noise that came to them through the motionless air could be called singing.

Carodoc said, "Evelake has gone to his hunting or fishing, else Annwyn would not be singing. Let us go."

The singing had stopped by the time they had made a wide circuit in order to come unseen upon the swineherd. He had slumped to the ground now. His eyes were shut and he seemed to be asleep. Ysobel thought he looked curiously defenseless and pathetic. She said softly, "It seems a pity to rouse him, Carodoc. I doubt he sleeps much at night for fear of Evelake."

"Yet, if we take away that fear, it will mean much to the poor manikin. Besides, we must rouse him, for who can say when Evelake will return?"

She sighed and agreed and they went quietly until they stood one on each side of the sleeper. Carodoc touched Annwyn's side with the soft toe of his shoe and the swineherd opened one eye and saw them and closed it again quickly, feigning sleep. Carodoc said, "Do not pretend, Annwyn. We know you are awake and we want to have speech with you."

The misshapen body upon the ground seemed to curl about itself like a hedgehog. Ysobel half expected it to roll away from them. She spoke gently. "Do not fear us, Annwyn. We will not harm you. We bring you good tidings."

There was no response, no sign of hearing or comprehending the words. Carodoc leaned over and caught Annwyn's shoulder and jerked him to his feet and held him firmly. "Listen to me, Annwyn. Listen. Do you know who I am? I am Carodoc, son of Abiris. I mean you no harm."

Still no response. Ysobel thought Annwyn might be a figure of wood without mind or spirit. Carodoc shook him roughly. "Hear me, Annwyn the Swineherd. Hear me and believe. Evelake is no god. He is but a man bent upon evil. He can do you no hurt. No hurt, do you hear, that I or any other man cannot do you. *Annwyn!*"

For a breathless second the day and the three of them seemed held in suspension as if it were a picture drawn upon a bit of bark. Then Annwyn came to life and spoke in a spate of broken words so mixed and tumbling it was almost impossible to make sense of them. Ysobel distinguished "Master" and "Lord of Darkness," but the rest was jumble. Carodoc shook him again and the words ceased. "The pin was a trick, Annwyn. A trick, do you hear? I could do it. You could do it. Even—even the Lady Ysobel could do it if she'd a mind to and knew the right place. Evelake—Evelake is no more than a *man*. A man, I tell you, like yourself. Like me. There are no gods but Beli. There is no Lord of Darkness."

He held his words, giving Annwyn time to understand what he had said, before he added, "What did you do in Carleon, Annwyn?"

Annwyn said, "No!" and waited and said, "Annwyn's Master is the Lord of Darkness. You . . . you . . . he will . . . he will *hurt* Annwyn." His voice rose in a high whine. "Tell them—tell them—tell them at the Henge, Annwyn. Burn fires. Burn fires. Burn. Bran. Warlock Bran. Thief Bran. Annwyn. Annwyn. Annwyn. Tell them. My Master. The Lord of Darkness. He will . . . he will . . . go away! Go away! Before he comes again."

Carodoc looked at Ysobel and saw in her as in a mirror the image of his own despair. They could not undo what Evelake had done. Not without more time. And they did not have time enough. They were only increasing Annwyn's terror now. His arms and legs were twitching, his body jerking, under Carodoc's strong grip.

Carodoc thought quickly. They could take no more time

here. The sun was already past the noonstead. Evelake might be back at any moment. Would Annwyn tell him of their visit? He doubted it, but he must make sure.

With his free hand he lifted Annwyn's shaking head and looked at him sternly. He lowered his voice until it was deep and full of mystery and repeated Latin words he'd learned from a Roman trader when he had gone to the West to buy tin. *"Gallia est omnes divisa in partes tres."* He wondered fleetingly what the words meant. The Roman trader had been interrupted before he could make them clear. "I have the power of spells, Annwyn." He was glad to see a spark of understanding in the fear-glazed eyes. "I do now put upon you the spell of silence. You cannot speak of me or the Lady Ysobel to your master. *Uno. Duo. Tres."*

He released Annwyn, hoping the nonsense he had spoken would keep their presence secret. Annwyn did not wait for more. He slid behind the golden bush and into the cave, trusting, Carodoc thought, in Evelake's special powers to keep them from following him.

Carodoc turned to Ysobel and they walked around the hill and across the downs. There was no need to speak of their failure with Annwyn, and they could not at once summon courage to examine together the full meaning of Annwyn's broken talk. Ysobel spoke of it first. She had to speak. The pressure of despair upon her was too great for longer silence.

"Will he accuse Bran of witchcraft and theft at the mid-summer fires?" She put it as a question, though there was, in truth, no question in her mind.

"Yes."

"All hope is lost, then."

Carodoc did not speak. She did not expect him to.

She wished she could spill the weight of her pain in tears and knew she could not. This day marked the end of their seeking for truth. Bran would die and she would die with him, though her body would live to walk through endless days and months and years, alone, until its appointed time for death. Already she could feel those years pressing heavily upon her.

Carodoc seemed to know her thoughts. "There is a way, Ysobel. There could, perhaps, be a way. But it is forbidden."

She scarcely heard him, and what little she heard had no meaning for her. She thought he was babbling to keep her from thinking her own thoughts.

He went on, talking aloud to himself. "If it were not forbidden, the ancient magic might reveal the truth. But it *is* forbidden."

Ancient magic. The words crept inside the numbness of her heart and lay there like inert logs beneath the lake village. They lay heavily, upon her heaviness, and she stirred her mind to be rid of them.

Ancient magic. Ancient magic. Ancient magic. The words swelled and beat upon her like the refrain of a song, singing in her ears until the crust of her self-absorption broke and she heard their meaning as well as their sound.

Carodoc's gift. The ancient secret power that he had, alone in his time and tribe, from their mother's people. She did not know, had never known, what this power was, only that Carodoc had it, knew he had it, and the Druids forbade its use. Carodoc, forcing their lagging steps to speed, sad of face and of heart—Carodoc had said something about his magic. He had said—*there was a way to help Bran, but it was forbidden.* He had said—*the ancient magic might reveal the truth if it were not forbidden.*

Forbidden by the priests. But they had no right to forbid the truth. Carodoc must forget them. He must do what they forbade him to do if there were a chance—even though the chance were no bigger than a seed of millet.

"Carodoc! Carodoc, you must use your secret magic. You must. You cannot let Bran die for Evelake's crime if there is a way—any way—to show the judges what is truth."

"Ysobel!" Her name was a cry and the cry revealed the agony of his own heart-struggle. "Do not torment me. It is forbidden. You know it is forbidden."

"Are you then afraid of the consequences to yourself? Would you let Bran die to save yourself the chastisement of Abiris?"

"No! No! No! It is not that. You know it is not that. I would gladly offer my own life for Bran's—and for your happiness."

This, she thought with pain, was no more than truth. She could not let him see her compassion. She could not let herself dwell upon it. Bran's life was in the balance.

"Then what do you fear?" she asked, and made the words sound cold and contemptuous.

"Fear! Nothing that man can do to me. But this—this thing is forbidden by the god himself. I cannot blaspheme the god."

"Forbidden by the god! Forbidden only by the *priests*, Carodoc. I doubt Beli came himself to you and set his prohibition upon you."

"By the priests. Yes. In Beli's name."

"In their *own* name, Carodoc. In their own interests. What good to your Beli"—she saw him look strangely at her and knew she had set herself at last, in very words, outside the beliefs of her people, and did not care—"to hide the truth? The priests have forbidden your magic for their own ends."

"Ysobel!"

His shocked whisper told her she had dented his

mind, and she went on. "Do you think their power over men would be so great if it were known that you and others like you, men who cannot even count their blood nine times pure, have this magic? Whence comes it except from the god? Would your Beli have given it to you if he had not expected you to use it in the cause of truth?"

"No," he said, and walked ten paces and said, "No," again, less doubtfully.

"Then let us go back, *now*, before it is too late, and use your power upon Annwyn."

"You do not understand, Ysobel. *If* I use it——"

She said quickly, "Not *if*, Carodoc. You *must* use it. You cannot let an innocent man die."

She wanted to turn away from the anguish of his mind, to close her ears against the broken thoughts that escaped in words he clearly did not know he spoke aloud. "The Druids. Priests of Beli. Is she right? Do they prohibit for their own ends? Blasphemy. I dare not blaspheme. But Bran is innocent. Bran must not die for Evelake. Oh! Evelake!"

The words ceased, but the struggle in him went on a little longer while she watched and pitied his suffering but could give her pity no rein. He said at last, reluctantly, so softly she could only just hear him, "You are right. I must try." She knew she had won. She knew he would not change his mind and, through surging relief, heard him say, "This you must know, Ysobel. It is not certain—I am not certain I can—can use the power sucessfully. It is not sure. I know I could not use it upon Evelake. With Annwyn there is a chance. But I must not try too soon. Annwyn will accuse Bran after sunrise at the Henge at Beli's stone. Then I must not come to him before sundown the night before. So long I know the power will hold—and I may not succeed, even with him. I have—I have never tested the power against —against a man."

She felt as if she had gone all the way to the Region of the Summer Stars and back again. She wondered if she could force her tired feet ahead. She looked about her and saw they were in their own familiar forest and heard a horse's whinny and took a little comfort thinking Caw had caught her scent and was greeting her.

"You can only try," she said and put her hand upon his arm and added, "Thank you, Carodoc."

CHAPTER FOURTEEN

THEY came to the Henge in the afternoon of midsummer eve. The wide green plain that topped the ridge above the river ran for leagues and would have dwarfed the mighty standing stones to disappoint the eye had not the mind remembered their majesty. The plain dwarfed, too, the thronging people of Britain until they seemed no more than swarming bees.

Ysobel had no heart for pleasure in the beauty before her when she and Carodoc led the village householders up the long hill to the plain. Somewhere nearby, but out of her sight, Bran would be preparing to wait out the last night of his life. Between him and disgraceful death stood only Carodoc and the strange power that had come to him from the dark ages before the great redheaded men had burst from the sea upon the land of Britain. If she could only go to Bran and comfort him! But Carodoc had said no one would be let near the prisoners.

Ysobel looked at her brother, riding with his head bent. He was, as he had been since they had tried with Annwyn and failed, silent and remote, withdrawn into himself, dedicated to the power within him. She had seen little of him during the days and nights between. He had spent most of them deep within the forest, where there was no one to distract his mind from his secret preparation for the task before him. Twice he had come back to the village and sought in his chest for something she had not seen and gone away again without speaking. He had grown thin and taut during those days and his eyes were deeper and blacker and more penetrating.

He turned aside from the trackway and led the small company to the place assigned to them. The others scattered quickly. Ysobel thought they were glad to be away from the tainted presence of two who, they suspected, would befriend a warlock. The villagers had ridden as far from the children of Abiris as they dared throughout the cheerless days upon the road. Ysobel thought they would have refused to be even so near had not the long rule of custom decreed it so.

Carodoc did not speak while they stowed their chests in the pavilion made ready for them and cleansed the road dust from their hands and faces. They were alone in the pavilion. Even Anya had become infected by the general fear of them and saw as little of them as she could.

They had made no plan for getting Evelake away from Annwyn, and as the sun drew closer to its setting Ysobel grew more and more strained. She must not think of Bran. She must hold her heart steady to do whatever she had to do. She did not know what that would be, though she had tortured her mind to think of a plan. Carodoc knew—she hoped.

"Ysobel."

His voice was, she thought, deeper and quieter and more vibrant than it had ever been before. It seemed almost to have taken on a life of its own separate from his life. It vibrated through the pavilion and through her nerve ends like a single harpstring. His power, she thought, must lie in that new voice and in his eyes. She looked at him, waiting, and saw or thought she saw what she had not seen before—a slight taut ridge across his forehead, as if a vein or a muscle pushed against his skin.

"Ysobel, you must keep Evelake away from Annwyn for one short hour."

She shuddered in revulsion at the thought of even a momentary nearness to Evelake and spoke, without thinking, out of that revulsion. "No. I—I cannot."

"You must. There is no other way. I cannot bind Annwyn to my will from afar. And there is no one else to help. You must—if Bran is to have a chance at life."

"How?"

"That I do not know. You must find a way."

"But I know of no way," she cried out in despair, and, in crying, knew what she must do and shrank from it.

Carodoc nodded, seeing the hateful knowledge grow in her. "Go, then. Evelake and Annwyn are twenty paces to the left and ten to the rear of this place. Evelake stands a little apart, watching Annwyn set up the pavilion. Get him away and keep him away until the last light has gone from the sky."

"How—how do you know these things?"

He made an impatient gesture with his shoulders. "It does not matter. Hurry."

She stared at him, almost fearing him, for another heartbeat and went from the pavilion and turned to the left.

She did not see the glory the sun threw like a mantle over the plain, turning it to a field of gold, or the dark, towering strength of Beli's stones. She was lonely and frightened, cut off from Bran, cut off even from Carodoc. Among the thousands of Britons, she walked apart, alone in a world of evil and terror. She would not be able to get Evelake

179

away. She would fail. Fail herself and Carodoc. Fail Bran. The fear of it beat in her mind.

She had come the twenty paces to the left and she turned and lifted her eyes and saw Evelake, his golden hair aflame in the light, his feet apart. As Carodoc had foretold, he was watching Annwyn, who struggled to lift the tent pole for a black pavilion shot with silver threads. Evelake's back was to her, but she knew as if she were beside him that he was laughing his evil, crystal laughter at Annwyn's struggles.

Her feet took root in the grassy lane. She could not come nearer. Fear and loathing rose in waves in her mind and filmed her eyes, and the taste of nausea filled her mouth. She could not do it, could not do the only thing that would induce Evelake to leave Annwyn for the necessary hour. She could not go to him and pretend to want his company. She could not pretend that she had deserted Bran and turned to Evelake as he had said she would. She could not use her deep woman's knowledge to snare his senses. Not when she loathed him and despised him and feared him.

If you love the good, there can be no fear. Love will drive out fear, yes, and all evil.

The words were as clear in her mind as if they had been spoken aloud. They had been her farewell from Joshua ben Joseph as they stood at the foot of the Tor—he and Bran and herself. She repeated them again and again, and as she said them a very power of love took her. Love for Bran and Carodoc; love for her father, Abiris, who she saw, flashingly, as she had seen him once before, as a man and not as a father and priest, doing at great pain to himself only what he thought right. She felt love for the terror-stricken Annwyn and even, in a strange way, for Evelake, who had abdicated his high duty as a leader to put on the mantle of pure evil. She looked about her and saw the beauty of the earth and the stones in their ordered plan and the motley-colored throng about her and loved them all.

She was no longer afraid. She would succeed in her errand. She would do what must be done for the needed hour. She walked briskly toward Evelake.

Carodoc waited where she had left him. The nerve that stood out upon his forehead throbbed steadily. He could see as if he had been with her each step of Ysobel's progress and he was filled with pity for her. Once he started toward the opening in the green tent and stopped himself with an effort and turned from it. Thereafter he waited, steadily. As she walked, at last, calmly and purposefully toward Evelake, Carodoc relaxed and the nerve ceased to throb. He took up a little basket fashioned of willow strips and covered with a white cloth and left the pavilion. He did not hurry, but neither did he dawdle. Like Ysobel, he walked blindly, deliberately shutting his senses away from the splendor that would assault them.

He turned into the lane between the pavilions where Ysobel had stood. Annwyn, alone, stared at the black and silver tent he had raised as if he could not quite believe his work was done. Carodoc began to hum softly, a lullaby he had learned from his mother, a gently, crooning, soothing sound that mingled in the soft midsummer wind with the smell of primroses and sweet grasses and the evening song of the larks.

Annwyn heard the melodies and felt the gentle, cooling air and smelled the scents. He turned slowly from the tent and for a moment his face was empty of terror.

He had not seen Carodoc, and Carodoc hurried a little as he went toward the swineherd, taking the white cover from the basket, still singing softly. He must, he thought, work quickly, before fear should again possess Annwyn.

The swineherd saw him and started to turn back to the safety of the tent. Carodoc called out a greeting, holding the basket for Annwyn to see. "Beli keep you, friend Annwyn. I have brought you a gift of mead and sweet honey cakes from our village in the lake." He was careful to keep his voice light and cheerful. He came on steadily. If he could reassure Annwyn, could convince him he came as a friend, his task would be easier.

Annwyn stood where he was, half turned away, held midway in his flight, his mind trying to grapple with this problem. He knew this man. He was Carodoc the Smith. His Master, the Lord of Darkness, had bade him keep away from every soul. But Carodoc was his master's friend. And there was mead. Mead for Annwyn. A gift. No one had ever brought him a gift of mead.

A silly, secret smile made slow progress over his face. By the April Rainers he was thirsty—thirsty for mead. His Master, the Lord of Darkness, had not let him have even a taste of mead since—since—he couldn't remember. He was tired of drinking water. There could be no harm in taking the gift. He started to stretch out his hand for the basket and remembered the terrible anger of his master and snatched his hand back.

Cardoc said, "It is good mead, Annwyn, rich with golden honey from the flowers of our Ynis Witrin." He pulled the wax cover from the flagon and held the basket closer to Annwyn. "Smell it. Savor its richness. Can you not feel the sun in it and hear the happy buzzing of the bees as they gathered the nectar? Take it. It is good."

The rich, heady smell tickled Annwyn's nose. His throat tingled with the thought of drinking. There could be no harm in it. His Master, the Lord of Darkness, was off with the Lady Ysobel. His master's mind would be busy with her. She would leave no part of it free to send prying into Annwyn's. His Master, the Lord of Darkness, would be too busy about his own affairs to know what Annwyn was doing. He would snatch the mead and run.

Carodoc saw the crafty look that came into the swineherd's eyes and tightened his hold upon the basket. Annwyn's long arm shot out toward it and Carodoc moved it until it was just beyond his reach. "I will bring the mead into the pavilion," he said, "where there will be none to see and come running to share its riches."

Annwyn hesitated yet another heartbeat, but his greed for the brew was too strong and he bobbed his head in acknowledgment and gestured to the tent opening in awkward mockery of a householder's offer of hospitality.

Carodoc stifled a sigh of relief and preceded the bent figure into the pavilion. He had succeeded in the first part of his task. He had overcome Annwyn's fear. The rest would be easier.

He watched quietly while Annwyn took the proffered flagon and lifted it to his mouth and drank deeply a full half of the mead in a single gulp. Annwyn looked at Carodoc and smiled his silly smile and smacked his lips. He held the flagon tightly with both hands, as if he feared it would be snatched away from him.

Carodoc smiled easily. "Let us talk a while, friend Annwyn, while you savor the drink." He saw terror begin to creep back into the crooked man and fight with his still unslaked thirst. "There is nothing to fear." Carodoc spoke softly, keeping his eyes on Annwyn's eyes. "Nothing to fear. Nothing to fear." His voice was slow and comforting. The sound of the words came gently—as gently as the sound of the lullaby. "You are weary, Annwyn, my friend. Weary. Weary. Weary. You would like to sleep. To sleep. To sleep."

Annwyn was relaxing. He swayed a little toward Carodoc and Carodoc said, "Sit upon the rushes, Annwyn. Sit and rest and do not fear. Drink the mead, Annwyn. Drink the mead. Drink. Drink. Drink."

Annwyn sighed deeply and sat on a pile of rushes not yet spread for Evelake's bed and drank the rest of the mead and set the empty flagon on the floor beside him, yawning a little. Carodoc took a rushlight and lit it at a clay brazier that held a little fire and held the light before Annwyn's eyes. "Look, my friend," he crooned. "Is not the flame a pretty thing? Watch it. Watch it. Watch it."

Annwyn watched the flame and, behind it, Carodoc's eyes, wide open and enormous. "You are tired, my friend. Your eyes are heavy. Your eyes are heavy. Your eyes are heavy. Heavy. Heavy. Heavy. They are closing. Closing. Closing. Sleep, Annwyn. Sleep. Sleep. Sleep."

He waited. Annwyn breathed regularly and easily. Carodoc touched his eyelids. He did not stir. The soothing voice said, "Are you asleep, Annwyn?"

Annwyn said, "I do be."

Carodoc, careful to let no change come into the measured rhythm, went on. "You will sleep for the quarter part of an hour. When you wake you will remember nothing of me or the mead or what we have said. On the morrow, when you speak at the judgment circle of Bran the Bard and the Arch Druid's egg, you will speak the truth and nothing else. You will say truly and fully all that befell you and Evelake and the guard Peredur and the egg upon the night it was stolen. You will name the true thief, no matter who he is. You will fear neither man nor god and you will know you will be safe from all harm. Safe. Safe. Safe."

His voice ceased its quiet melody. Annwyn said, "I hear, Carodoc the Smith, and I will obey."

Carodoc put the rushlight back in its place, picked up the flagon, and returned it to the basket beside the honey cakes, which he had not given Annwyn, having had no need to, and slipped out into the afterglow of the sunset. He was tired, but his mind felt light. He had done what he could. The rest belonged to the god.

He walked rapidly away from the black and silver pavilion toward the Fair Field, already alive with traders calling their wares. When he came to a stream at the foot of the plain, he took the flagon and dipped it again and again into the swift, flowing water until he was satisfied it was clean of all traces of the herb he had put into Annwyn's mead. He stopped a mead peddler and gave him a small silver coin to refill the flagon and, with it again in the basket, went to look for Ysobel, not wanting her to remain with Evelake a moment longer than was necessary.

Ysobel had been standing with Evelake near a booth, where they had stopped for honey cakes and slices of wild swan sizzling from a brazier. Evelake had eaten the food like a hungry animal, but Ysobel could not force herself to swallow and had walked away from the food vendor with the dripping meat making a sodden mess of the honey cake.

She was more frightened than she had ever been in her life, frightened of the look in Evelake's eyes, of his restless hands and caressing words. Where was Carodoc? The last light was fading. In a moment the dark would come down and enclose her with this man beside her. For the hour Carodoc needed she had turned aside Evelake's promises and endearments with teasing banter. For a time he had been content to play at the game of courtship, being sure of her in his mind. But he was no longer in a playful mood. He was angry and restless and a little suspicious. She could feel these things through the hand that gripped her arm above the elbow and see them, in the last of the light, upon his face, flushed with something she would not name. And she was spent. She had used all her reserves of deceit and she felt weak and tired, as if the blood in her veins had turned to honey and moved as slowly as honey through them.

"Ysobel, are you tricking me for some secret purpose of your own? If you are, woman, if you are——"

She hurried to interrupt him. "I am but weary, Evelake. The day—the day has been long."

She felt his grip upon her arm lessen somewhat, though he did not release her. "Come, then. We will go to the trysting place and declare our troth. I am in no mood for waiting."

She must find a way to distract him. She sought for words and knew none strong enough to stop him and said weakly, "First we must find Abiris."

He shook her arm so furiously she dropped the honey cake and the meat. "Abiris! What has Abiris to do with me? You are but playing with me and I will not have it. Do you hear? I will not have it. You will come with me to the trysting place now or——"

She had to get away from him. She had somehow to break free and run and lose herself in the night. She could hold him off no longer. "Let go my arm, Evelake," she said, trying to keep her voice from breaking. "You are hurting me."

"I'll hurt you more, woman, if you do not——"

"Well met, Evelake, and well met, Ysobel. I have been seeking you, my sister, to bid you eat, not knowing you were occupied with so good a friend."

Ysobel almost lost her senses at the sound of Carodoc's

voice. She took a stumbling step toward him as Evelake straightened and dropped her arm, and she leaned against her brother, dizzy with relief.

Evelake said nastily, "Carodoc. Must you always appear when you are least wanted? Or is this a trick to keep me from the Lady Ysobel?"

Carodoc laughed lightly. "A trick, Evelake? I do not understand. Why should I trick you, my friend? Come, let us walk together, we three, back to the pavilions, for it is growing late and there'll be little enough sleep for any of us this night."

He took Ysobel's arm and urged her along a lane, feeling her shaking and pressing her a little to reassure her. Evelake came with them. His angry suspicion was as evident as if they could see his face. Carodoc paid no attention to it. He told a long, rambling tale about a cross-eyed, knock-kneed fellow who had forced upon him a flagon of mead, begging him to sample the brew and tell his friends of its merits. He was an excellent teller of tales and an excellent mimic and by the time he had done Ysobel had all but forgotten her fear and even Evelake was laughing and relaxed again.

When they came within sight of the black and silver tent, Annwyn was standing before it as she had left him an hour ago. She saw the old terror upon his face as he ducked inside the opening and her heart sank, for she thought Carodoc had failed in whatever he had set out to do and her own trial had been useless. But Carodoc pressed her arm steadily and she admonished her untrusting heart, knowing he had not failed. She smiled at Evelake and agreed easily that she would see him on the morrow.

He left them then and Carodoc hurried her to their own pavilion and, in its secrecy, told her he had bound Annwyn to his will—but whether the bonds would hold until the morrow, he could not say. He brought her food and bade her sleep a while which, scarcely believing it possible, she did—more deeply and quietly than she had for many nights.

A quarter league away, Bran watched the sun sink upon his life. From the hill, where he stood inside the wicker cage, he could see, as he had seen each year, the circles of stones that were the most sacred fane in all the world that worshiped Beli. He would go there tomorrow in the deep night hour that foretold the dawn, not singing as a bard, but herded like an animal beside his cage.

This night he would not sleep. He would examine his heart for the last time as he had examined it many times since the Beltane. The hope that had come to him when the boy had brought Carodoc's message in Carleon had died slowly as the days marched toward midsummer and he remained a prisoner, but the memory of hope had stiffened his heart and he had not again sunk into blank melancholy. He had instead used slow-moving time to look into his mind and study himself, as in a well of clear water.

All his life he had been like a child, cared for and protected, helped along a way made smooth by Abiris the Druid. And, like a child, he had been content to let dark doubts be vanquished by any chance and soothing word. He had been a fool, he had thought bitterly; and for a time he had known only scorn and disgust for himself and had given up searching his heart. But by little and little he had come again to it, since he had had nothing else to distract his mind from the fires of the Henge.

As he sat now in the cage on this last midsummer eve of his life and watched the afterglow fade into night and Beli's dark stones lose their outlines, he felt a strange kind of peace. He could look steadily at the evil that walked the world of men and accept it, for he knew that evil must ever be the handmaiden of good. He knew, too, that truth was more than words or deeds. Truth ran deep and still within each man, like the blue water of the River Brue that ringed the foot of the Tor at Ynis Witrin. It must be sought and captured and held fast in loneliness—each man by himself with his own truth in the secret place of his heart.

What was *his* truth, he wondered. He could not tell. He thought wistfully he would not now have time to find it out. A man might spend three score years and still not be sure. He would not live as many hours. He knew but one small part of his own truth. It had nothing to do with Beli or Beli's priests. He had examined all his past doubts about the Druids as he waited, and faced them honestly and fully and known them justified. There had been, he did not doubt, a time when the Druid order was a splendid thing and needful for the strengthening of a people freshly come to a new land. But, as the power of the priests had grown, so had their arrogance and their misuse of power.

The god? What was Beli now but a tool of his priests? Who could say what the god was like apart from the men who served him? If he was as dark and cruel and evil as the Druids made him, he was not worthy of such service as Bran the Brave had given him in his heart. A god without compassion and love for his people, a god who wanted sacrifices and more sacrifices from them, was no god at all. There was—there must be—some other deity like the one served by Joshua ben Joseph perhaps, but there was no time now to seek him.

Tomorrow, very early in the first watch after midnight, they would come and take him to the river and wash him clean and take his rags and give him decent clothes. They would cleanse his cage and he would walk beside it along the Processional Way, bound by leather thongs, guarded by archers and spearmen and swordsmen, a common criminal going to his final judgment. Tomorrow.

Somewhere in the distance he heard the steady tread of the changing watch. No longer tomorrow. Today.

He had but a few heartbeats of time to think now. Had he, then, found anything else of his truth in those long, hideous days? He did not know. His mind was empty.

Time for thinking had run out. His final guard was beside the cage. He looked out at them and saw them led by Gwyth, his tormentor, and felt the beginning of the old shivering fear and looked into the red, hating eyes of Gwyth. Gwyth opened the cage door and dragged him roughly out, threatening him with the rod. Bran lifted his head to the night sky, stretching his back for the blows if they should come, not cowering. He drew in his breath deeply and looked into Gwyth's face and spoke to him. "Good morrow, brother."

Gwyth's mouth opened in wonder and he dropped the rod to his side and stammered, "Good—good morrow, Bran."

Bran lifted his clear voice and sang softly into the night a wordless melody of rejoicing. He had discovered one more part of his own truth—or rediscovered it. He was, indeed, Bran the Brave, and he could endure what must be endured this day with dignity and fortitude. He turned his back upon the guard and walked unfettered toward the river, and no man tried to restrain him.

CHAPTER FIFTEEN

TEN thousand people of the tribes of Britain waited in the darkness upon the great plain of the Henge for the moment of sunrise upon midsummer day. The sound of their quiet talk rose and fell as the waves of the great sea upon a windless day. Above them the bowl of the sky turned slowly, almost imperceptibly, from night blue to milky white. The mighty stones in Beli's Great Circle emerged as shadows, then as sharp black outlines beyond the bank and ditch that set them apart. The empty gash of the Processional Way wound upward from the river to the circle, splitting the waiting thousands into two throngs. Just short of the ditch it divided around the Sunstone, which stood alone, more than twice the height of a man.

Ysobel, so near the Sunstone she could almost reach out and touch it, saw, as the light strengthened, each Druid, each bard and ovate, motionless in his place within the Great Circle, eyes fixed upon the Arch Druid. He, too, stood motionless—at the head of the dread recumbent altar stone, the stone of sacrifice. She could see the sword he held by the point to show he was ready to die for truth and, beside him, a goat trussed for the sacrifice.

The milky heavens began to flush with dawn and the

murmuring of the people died into a silence that swept back and back until it reached and held the lowliest villein at the edge of the crowd. The tribes turned as one person toward the east and waited.

Beyond the plain's end, at the horizon, the sun appeared as a thin red line above the green earth. It rose slowly and slowly, higher and higher. For a moment it seemed to rest upon the rim of the world before it flamed clear and showed its orb, complete but a little flattened by the air, balanced exactly upon the apex of the Sunstone, touching with reflected crimson light the altar of sacrifice and the face of the Arch Druid.

The bards swept their harps and Ysobel thought it was as if the sun itself had brought into being the fall of sweet sound. The bards sang the first line of the hymn to the sun and ten thousand voices took up the canticle and sent their praise of the light and warmth that brought life to all growing things ringing to the very height of heaven.

Ysobel did not join in the singing. She felt no awe save for the awe that lies in all beauty, no reverence except reverence for the knowledge and skill of ancient men that had so precisely set the Sunstone to catch and hold the sun itself upon its rising on midsummer day. She wanted to pray with the others, but she could not. Beli was the only god she knew, and he lay dead in her heart, because he demanded the sacrifice of men in return for his gifts.

She could not pray to him. Yet she needed to pray, needed help from somewhere outside herself, to endure the ordeal of Bran's trial that was coming. There were, she had been told, other gods. Somewhere there must be a god of justice and mercy and love, a god who did not require death as a price for his goodness to men. If she could speak to such a god, he would surely ease her pain and send her strength for what was to come.

She remembered the god of Joshua ben Joseph. He, too, if she had understood aright, was a god of light. If she could only reach him with her prayers! But he had in this land no altar and no name. Very well. Since she had no god of her own, she would make an altar in her heart to the compassionate god of Joshua ben Joseph and his people and name him the Unknown God and ask his help.

The singing had ceased. The people were quiet, rapt in watching the priests at their sacrifices within the circle. Ysobel closed her eyes and set her thoughts upon her Unknown God.

Carodoc's voice startled her from her silent communion. "Come, Ysobel. They have finished, and Bran will come first to judgment."

The Druids had left the circle and were going, more quickly than usual, toward a space set apart for judgment a little distance from the Processional Way. Carodoc hurried her after them and pushed a path through the silent, somber people, until he brought them to the forefront of the crowd.

The Arch Druid waited, surrounded by a hundred white-robed figures, in the center of the cleared space. Behind them, in ranks of massed green and blue, the ovates and bards stood still as the stones they had left. A squad of spearmen, their spears locked in a firm line, kept a space cleared between the Druids and the people. Their straight, taut backs and the rigid wall of ash struck at Ysobel like a physical blow, and she twisted her head away from them and looked toward the far-reaching, level stretches of purple-shadowed grass and caught the first sight of a moving column of soldiers—archers, swordsmen, spearmen—and, in their midst, a great wicker cage, with Bran walking before it, tethered to it with strong leather thongs. She thought she gave a cry of anguish, but no sound came from her. She felt the blood draining from her head and knew she was falling and felt Carodoc's arms about her and fought the faintness of her spirit.

"Courage, Ysobel. Look again at Bran and take strength from him." She thought she could not do as Carodoc bade her. She closed her eyes hard and swallowed and the swimming in her head stopped and she stood free of his arm and straight and looked at Bran.

For a moment she thought she had lost her wits or that this man who walked erect and strong and proud could not be a prisoner. He was dressed in gray, dull breeches and a loose shirt like a villein. His hair, grown over the tonsure, was bright in the sun above a face that was lean and taut and seemed miraculously free from care or suffering or fear. This was the face of a man grown into understanding so deep it could not know fear—not the boyish, trusting face she had known so long.

She had no time to speak to Carodoc, no time to ponder upon the change in Bran. The marching line had come to the center of the judgment space and halted. Bran stood looking steadily at the people before him. He found Ysobel and Carodoc and smiled at them and the smile, full of love and faith and strength, tore at her heart. She raised her hand and forearm in salute, though she could no longer see him clearly for tears.

An ovate stepped forward beside the Arch Druid and began to recite the charges of witchcraft and sacrilegious theft against the prisoner. Ysobel felt a touch upon her arm and looked around and saw Evelake, with Annwyn beside him, and drew herself away, shrinking against Carodoc on her other side. Evelake seemed not to notice her shrinking. He stooped and brought his lips close to her ear and whispered, "Soon, my lady, soon." Someone hissed at him for silence and he straightened away from her and she breathed again.

The ovate finished the charges and the Arch Druid said in a voice so low Ysobel could hardly hear it, "Are these things true, Bran the Brave, upon your strong oath as a free man?" and Bran looked into his eyes and said in his bard's trained voice, loud and clear, quickly, firmly, "No!"

The Arch Druid looked as if he did not believe his own ears. Few prisoners had the strength and courage to deny such charges or to stand so straight or look so true. He waited a full minute, watching Bran, willing him to change his word so that the trial—if such it could be called—could be quickly finished. Bran did not take his eyes from the Arch Druid's eyes, did not move, did not speak again, and the Arch Druid shifted uneasily and said, "Who sayeth otherwise?"

There was a restless movement in the crowd and a murmuring as of aspen leaves stirred by a summer breeze. Someone behind her jostled Ysobel and another said, "Move over, lady. Let this man through," but before she could move, Abiris had come forward beside the Arch Druid. Ysobel had not seen him since the Beltane and she caught her breath at the change in him. His auburn hair was streaked with white and his face was lined and heavy. But his voice came strong as a trumpet as he looked at the hostile crowd.

"I, Abiris the Druid, do stand forth and say the charge of witchcraft is *false,* and I demand in the name of justice and the love of justice, which is the love of good, that Bran the Brave be discharged of this crime against the god, Beli, and against the tribes of this land."

The crowd howled and pushed at the locked spears. "Warlock! Warlock! Warlock! Burn him! Burn him! Burn him!" they shouted, angry that their sport was threatened.

Within the circle of the bards and ovates someone blew a great blast upon a horn and the Arch Druid raised his hands commanding silence. The crowd, obedient to his authority, leashed its tongue and the Arch Druid said, "You have sure knowledge, Abiris the Druid?"

"Sure knowledge. I have diligently searched out each suspicion of witchery as it is ordered and have found no sign of true spells. Three things were named against Bran the Warlock. A cow would not give milk. A man child was stricken dumb and motionless. A field of corn would not come to ear. I, Abiris, say to you, Arch Druid, and to you, people of the tribes of Britain, these accusations are not true. The cow was ill-favored and weakly. She belonged to a slattern, more eager for mead than for milk. The animal had fed upon tares and drunk marsh water. At my command it was taken from the woman and fed good grain and sweet water. It is today sleek and fat and giving milk, and to these words I can bring witnesses upon oath."

The people shifted restlessly, but there was less grumbling, and Ysobel heard some who already thanked Beli that there was no warlock among them. She looked at Evelake and saw him black with anger and knew he had indeed started the rumors of witchcraft.

Bran's face did not alter as Abiris disproved the other slanders. The man child had been willful and disobedient. Punished by his father, he had pretended to be witched until his frightened parents had given him his way. The corn that would not come to ear had been planted late, in poor soil, by a careless husbandman. After each statement, Abiris repeated, "And to these words I can bring witnesses upon strong oath."

When he came to the end of his declarations he turned to

face the Arch Druid. "I, Abiris the Druid, do now declare all charges of witchcraft against Bran, the Prisoner, false and full of malice. I do demand, in justice, that he be separated from the burning cage forever," and the Arch Druid bent his head and said, "Let it be done."

One of the guards took a bronze knife from his belt. The sun flashed on the blade as it cut through the thong that tethered Bran to the cage. Two other guards tested the knots that held his hands together, tight behind his back, and fastened other thongs to his feet to hobble them. Through it all, Bran made no move nor changed the set look upon his face.

Carodoc said, "Thanks to Beli, he is safe from the burning," and Ysobel answered, "Thanks only to Abiris, who is just. There is still the charge of sacrilege and theft."

Evelake laughed softly beside her. "Do not fear, my lady. The charge of thievery will not so quickly be dismissed."

Hatred for him surged within her. She drew her hands into fists to beat his grinning mouth and felt Carodoc holding her with all his strength and heard his soft command, "No," and opened her hands again.

The Arch Druid said, "There is yet the charge of theft of the sacred jewel. Speak it forth again," and Evelake whispered gleefully, "*Now* it comes, my lady."

The ovate recited again the full tale of the theft and the evidence against the prisoner. The Arch Druid again asked Bran upon his oath if the charges were true and Bran again said, "No," loud and clear.

Quickly, upon Bran's denial, Carodoc spoke out from his place. "I, Carodoc, free man of the tribe and son of the Druid Abiris, say the charge of theft is *not proven*."

The Arch Druid looked as if he had been struck by Beli's lightning. He was not accustomed to being challenged by a mere craftsman, and for a moment his usually calm face showed anger. What would he do? Ysobel wondered. Would he send his guard to seize Carodoc? Would he——

Evelake shouted, "I, Evelake the Wise, say otherwise, and I have here a witness to prove my truth." He pushed Annwyn to the barrier of locked spears. "Annwyn, the Swineherd, will give you sure proof."

The Arch Druid said, "Let Annwyn, the Swineherd, come before me."

Annwyn cowered under Evelake's hand upon his shoulder. One of the spearmen grounded his spear and Evelake pushed Annwyn through the opening in the ash wall. The swineherd stumbled and fell to his knees before the Arch Druid, who leaned forward and helped him to his feet, speaking soothingly and quietly to him.

Ysobel thought the pressures of hope and fear within her would choke her. She turned to Carodoc for comfort and found him gone and looked wildly about for him. She saw him, stooping through the crowd, his knife in his hand, circling toward Bran. She guessed he was afraid of what Annwyn would say and hoped by some magic or miracle to cut Bran's bonds, that he might escape if Annwyn failed.

Bran's guards had been caught up in the drama of Carodoc's challenge and Evelake's answer. They had relaxed their watchfulness. Their bowstrings were slack, the arrows pointing harmlessly toward the earth. They were watching Annwyn, not Bran. Carodoc, free of the crowd, moved behind the guard, coming closer to Bran.

Ysobel felt a coldness in her as she imagined Carodoc's scheme. She thought he would try to take advantage of the inattention of the guards and cut Bran's leg bonds, hoping he would win to freedom in the following confusion. He could be right, she thought. But if he were, if he could free Bran, what, then, of himself? If Bran escaped, Carodoc's life would be forfeit. She started to call out to him and stopped herself, fearing to call attention to him, fearing that the very intention to free a god-dedicated prisoner would bring instant death. She looked away, setting her whole attention upon Annwyn.

He stood beside the Arch Druid. He was no longer cowering and shivering. He had found a kind of dignity of his own and there was nothing in his face of strain or fear.

"Speak, Annwyn the Swineherd. Speak loud and clear that all may hearken to the truth of Bran, the Prisoner, and the chevron bead." The Arch Druid put his hand upon the bent shoulder beside him.

In short, clear sentences Annwyn told of his coming to Carleon with Evelake and of all that had happened there on the day before the theft. Evelake put his arm about Ysobel's shoulder and drew her to him. "Now," he whispered; "now it comes. The proof. And we shall be free of Bran forever."

Her whole being was so centered upon Annwyn's next words she did not hear Evelake or feel his detested touch. What the swineherd said next would free Bran or sign his death.

Annwyn took his time. The words came deliberately, as if he would be altogether sure of them, almost as if he spoke without knowing it. "My master went a little from the town of Carleon to a secret place he knew of, and I with him, and we waited through a night and a day."

The crowd pushed forward. This was not what they had expected to hear, not what they had been told. Evelake tried to give Annwyn some sign, but Annwyn paid no heed. He was looking above their heads as if he saw the things he spoke of in the sky itself. Evelake shouted, "Annwyn!" The swineherd turned a wooden face toward him and away again and went on with his story.

"When it neared dusk the next night, my master gave me a packet of blue cloth and three silver coins and told me to go to the house of the Arch Druid and, taking care that I was not discovered, give the packet to one whose name was Tostig, who would be hidden in a certain clump of elder-bushes that grew hard by the kitchen. My master said I was to wait in those same bushes when Tostig was gone until my master came to me, and this I did, and was near discovered when one in the town cried out an alarm and the high captain made search—though it was raining—but I covered myself with leaves and lay still and the high captain passed me by, swearing great oaths."

Ysobel's heart was singing. Carodoc had succeeded in what he had set out to do. Annwyn was telling the truth—all of it. Bran was as good as free already. She slid a glance at Evelake and saw his face white as the Arch Druid's robe and his eyes wild with fear. He twisted about and tried to break through the people behind him, but they were packed close and tight and they would not yield a way for him. He put his hand to the band of his breeches and took out a knife and held it close to his side. She wondered what he intended to do but would not take her mind away from Annwyn to reckon further.

"My master came soon then and led me by twisting ways into the Arch Druid's house and to the room where the high captain made talk with Bran the Bard and we waited, concealed by a roof post, in the shadows until Bran had left and, after him, a man with a scarred face. And still we waited for a little and a little, and then my master bade me go into the room and take from the high captain the great key that unlocked the little door of the treasury and get the Arch Druid's egg and bring it to him and this I did for fear of my master, who is the Lord of All Evil, and we went away into the forest, leaving the high captain sleeping sound."

"Lies!" Evelake shouted. "All lies." He tried again to make a way through the people behind, but they hemmed him in, muttering against him.

The Arch Druid's voice was a bellow as he ordered silence and turned again to Annwyn. "Where is the chevron bead, Annwyn the Swineherd?"

Annwyn looked at him stupidly and the priest repeated, a little testily, "The Arch Druid's egg, Annwyn. Where is it now?"

"Sewn in my master Evelake's tunic," Annwyn said, and Ysobel felt herself seized roughly and heard Evelake's voice hissing in her ear. "Do not move, betrayer. My knife point is against your heart."

He began to move backward, dragging her with him, holding her as a shield for his body. She could feel the people nearest them give way, seeing her plight, and she was afraid.

The Arch Druid said, "Bring me Evelake, the Thief," and Evelake shouted, "No! Touch me and Ysobel, daughter of Abiris, dies! Make way! Make way! Make way!"

CHAPTER SIXTEEN

EVELAKE, still holding her in painful grip, turned with her until his back was to the congregation of the Druid Order. She could see her own fear and her own horror reflected in the eyes of the people who opened a silent path before them. Evelake pushed her ahead of him toward the Processional Way, stretching empty to the river. Would he drive the knife into her heart once he was upon a clear road or would he wait until he had forced her the long, long way to its end? Once he gained the river, he had a chance for freedom. She thought of Bran and tried to twist her head for one more look at him and felt the knife prick through her tunic and cried his name in her heart in a despairing last farewell, for she knew she would die when Evelake no longer needed her.

Behind her there was no sound. Neither the priests nor the people dared move for certainty that Evelake would kill her at once. Only Bran, though she could not hear him, with the cage at his back, spoke to Carodoc, bidding him cut the leather thongs, and Carodoc, released to action by the words, did so. Bran seized the drooping bow and arrow from the nearest guard and caught the strong web of the cage and climbed steadily, knowing at last the full evil of Evelake, who had been his friend, praying that the wicker would hold.

The guard, after a startled and witless look at his empty bow hand, went after him. Carodoc barred the way, his knife at the guard's throat, a hand clamped against the guard's mouth to keep back any warning cry. "Let him alone, you fool," Carodoc said into the guard's ear. "He only seeks to save the girl. He will not escape. Why should he, since he is proved innocent of crime?"

Bran reached the top of the cage. He gave no attention to the guard and Carodoc, though a part of his mind knew what was happening below him. He kept his eyes on Evelake, calculating his progress and the distance and the force and direction of the light breeze that blew across the uplands. He brought the bow up steadily, the arrow held taut against the bowstring. He put all the strength of his arms and shoulders against the pull of the yew and bent it into an arch and held it until Evelake broke through the fringe of the crowd on to the Processional Way, empty of people, since it was sacred to the god. He released the arrow and watched its swift, clean flight and wondered if the distance would reduce its striking power too greatly. Then he saw both Evelake's hands fly out as he felt the bite of the tip, saw the knife that had threatened Ysobel flash in the sun as it spun in a long arc out of the hand, saw Ysobel drop to the ground as the restraining arm fell from her, and saw Evelake, the arrow shaft still quivering in his back, begin to run. Bran stayed for one other moment atop the cage that might have been his funeral pyre until the crowd moved, some to go to Ysobel, others to cut off Evelake and surround him. Then weak, as if his body had been drained of all its strong-flowing blood, he began to climb down the side of the cage. Almost at once arms supported him and he looked down and saw Carodoc just beneath him, staying his trembling, helping him to the firm, good earth.

He drew in breath after breath of the clear, clean air, having time now to know he was no longer a prisoner, no longer named thief and warlock. The calm that had held him deserted him and he began to shake. Carodoc pounded his back and spoke encouragement and the shaking went away and he became aware of the confusion all about him, of shouts in the crowd and movement among the guards, who had formed ranks and were marching double-quick toward the Processional Way. He said, "Ysobel?" and it was Abiris who answered him, Abiris with his shoulders straight and his face lighted with relief and happiness.

"Safe, Bran," Abiris said. "They are bringing her now to us." The happiness went away from his eyes and he said, "Bran. Bran. Dare I seek your forgiveness for mistrust? I do not——"

Bran cut short his protestations. He had no mind to hear them now or ever. Forgive? He would surely forgive Abiris, but it would, he thought, be many moons before the memory that Abiris had believed him guilty would leave his mind. To speak the words of forgiveness was easy, but to forget the hurt to his own love for his foster father—that was something else, something he thought he could not do. "Let be, Abiris. You did what you must and it is over now and finished. Let us not speak of it again." Abiris, knowing himself rebuked, knowing he deserved it, said, "So be it."

Carodoc broke the tension between them that had followed upon Abiris' words. "They come, Bran, with Ysobel," Carodoc said and pointed to a little group of men before whom the people gave way. One of the group carried Ysobel in his arms as if she were a baby, and Bran, seeing her still and limp, cried out despairingly, "She is dead. He killed her before he dropped the knife."

The man who held Ysobel began to protest and Ysobel opened her eyes and saw Bran beside her and smiled a little thin smile at him and said, "Not dead, Bran; only—only near witless with fright."

He took her then from the man who had brought her and cradled her against his shoulder and crooned to her a wordless melody of love. He brought her to the judgment place and laid her upon the grass and sent one of the boys for water. When the boy came back with a brimming amber cup, she sat up and drank, resting her back against Bran's arm. There were so many things she wanted to say to him— but not here; not in this crowd; not with Abiris watching, his eyes so sad they would never again dance with the unforgotten gaiety of his youth; not with the Arch Druid hovering to make his apologies and what restitution he could to Bran the Bard. "Take me away, Carodoc," she whispered to her brother. And when Bran protested he would take her, she shook her head at him. "You cannot, beloved. Not yet. The Arch Druid is impatient and they—they will surely want you for—for Evelake's . . ." Her voice drifted into silence and she watched him, fearing to see pain in his eyes. He looked calmly at her, the strength of mind and heart he had found in the days of his prisonment steady in him. "Yes," he said. "Evelake. Do not grieve for me on his account, my birdling." His expression changed and showed bitterness and he went on. "One man's fall from goodness is only a little thing amidst so many evils."

Ysobel sighed. She thought, he must not carry bitterness in his heart, though he is, of all men, justified in feeling bitter against his kind. But bitterness could spoil a whole lifetime if it was let to continue. She said, "Oh, Bran, do not——" but he was smiling at her again, as if he knew what she was about to say. "Do not fear for me, Ysobel," he whispered. "I am not truly angered. Not for long. Do you go now with Carodoc and I will come when all—all this is finished."

The sun set before he came, washed and combed and resplendent in scarlet tunic and breeches he had borrowed from someone. She, too, was freshly dressed in her best gown with her finest torque of silver enameled in red, setting off the soft blue of her mantle. She had eaten and slept, and showed no sign of the moments when death had been but a little away. Their meeting was solemn and restrained with a shyness that came between them for a reason she could not name. The day had been full of so many emotions they could not meet lightheartedly. He held her briefly in his arms and kissed her once before he sat a little apart from her upon a hummock of grassy earth.

He seemed to her drawn into himself, deliberately holding his mind and heart from her, and she felt chilled and lonely. She asked him of Evelake and he told her calmly, remotely, that Evelake's arrow wound had been poulticed with mistletoe against poison, that he was being held under guard until the wound had healed. He told her Evelake was as a man bereft of his senses, staring about him with eyes that seemed blind while a froth spumed from his mouth and fell upon his splendid torque unnoticed.

"What will happen to him, Bran?"

Bran did not know. When the Druids questioned him, he had told all he knew of Evelake since his failure to pass the bard's test. Ganhelon had come before the priests and pleaded for his son's life. Evelake himself would not speak but lay upon a heap of rushes not knowing that the men who watched him were guards or that he was a prisoner.

The priests might have him killed. Or they might send him out of the land of Britain forever. No man could know their minds.

"And Annwyn?" Ysobel hoped the poor crooked man would take no harm for his part in the theft.

"Oh, Annwyn," Bran answered, and smiled a little. "He will come to no harm. It was plain Evelake had so filled his weak mind with terror he could not be held blameworthy. The Druids tried to find out what had freed him to tell truly all that took place, but Annwyn could do no more than shake his head and smile his silly smile. Carodoc has promised to be responsible for Annwyn. Carodoc declares he will use him as helper in the forge, though why he should do so I know not."

She started to tell him that Carodoc had used his ancient power to force the truth from Annwyn and thought this was Carodoc's secret and must not be shared even with Bran, whose life it had saved, unless Carodoc chose to tell it himself. "It is a mystery," she agreed. "But Carodoc doubtless has his own reasons. He was ever kind and compassionate to all weak creatures."

Bran got up and made a light against the gathering night and sat down again. Outside the tent the voices of the villeins bustling about the evening meal made a cheerful sound, but within there was only silence. When she could no longer bear the quiet and the feeling of separation between them, Ysobel spoke his name, calling out to him to break the barrier.

He half got to his feet and sat back again and said calmly and remotely, "Yes, Ysobel?" and she fought against the threat of tears until her voice was schooled to steadiness and said, "What is it, Bran? Why are you so—so far from me? You have been close to dying, as I have been, this day, and now we are safe and should rejoice in full happiness that we can start our life together. But you—you are as a stranger. What has come to you that you set me apart from you? Have I then gained your life only to lose your love?"

"Oh, Ysobel." Her name was wrenched from him in a cry of despair that left her shaken and more uncertain than before. She waited for him to say more, but he only put his head between his two hands and rocked it from side to side. The rushlights glowed upon the scarlet of his breeches and she became aware, for the first time, that he was not wearing his bard's robe and she got up from the ground and came and stood above him.

"Bran! They have not—they *could* not—refuse to restore your bardship to you?"

He lifted his head and looked at her then and words rushed from him as water rushes down a mountainside in the spring floods. "Refused? No. They have not refused. It is I who refused to return to their company. It is as if—as if there had been scales upon my eyes. For all the years of my living I have believed their teachings, believed in their God of Light, their Beli. I have worshiped him in my heart and in the sacred groves and followed the ways of his priests and beaten down the doubts I once told you of."

He stood up and took her face in his hands and looked into her eyes. "If you could only know, Ysobel. If there were only some way I could tell you. If your heart and mind, which are good and pure, could only know the great, stalking evil things that power can bring to men who have too much of it. Even Abiris—Abiris, whom I have loved and cherished all the days of my life; Abiris, who found me, kin-shattered and landless, and took me for his own to keep me safe—even Abiris is not proof against this evil. I had many hours for thinking, Ysobel, there in my cage at Carleon. I tell you the Order of the Druids is dying—dying of its own decay. Beli! Beli is no more than a—an excuse to them now—an excuse to keep the people of this land in bondage to the fear of the Druids. Could you only know—how can I make you know and understand what I have done?"

She said quietly, "I do know, Bran. I do understand. I, too, have had time to think and to—to question."

He looked at her in a kind of wonder. "Then—you do not blame me over much, my Ysobel, that I cannot return to their priesthood and their god?"

"I do not blame you, Bran. There are—there must be—other gods. Gods of love and compassion. We will seek them together." Time enough later to speak of her Unknown God.

"We?" She saw despair take him again. "We? There can be no *we,* my birdling, ever again."

She took his shoulders in her hands and shook them a little. "What are you saying, Bran? What do you mean there can be no we?"

"You are not thinking, Ysobel. I have denied the Druids. I have left the order of the bards. I will go no more to study in the oak grove with Abiris. And I am a kin-shattered man. I am not like to Evelake with lands and cattle, silver coins and hunting hounds, for my portion. I have no land. I have not even clothes to my back save only these that are borrowed. I must spend my life upon the road, a beggar or, at best, since I have still some knowledge of the trickery of hand and eye and a voice to sing, a wandering gleeman at the fairs, working my tricks and singing my songs for the amusement of the people who delight to be fooled and for what crusts and bones they will give me."

She looked at him steadily. "What has that to do with me? My legs are strong and my heart. I have no land, being a woman—nor will ever have. But I have a heritage of kine from my mother. I will wander with you."

He smiled bleakly. "No. For the present, while we are young and strong, when the sun is warm and food plentiful, we two could go blithely enough from Fair Field to Fair Field. But there are other years and other seasons. No, Ysobel, without land, without a settled place, without kin at his back to fight his battles, a man must live in loneliness and hopelessness and I will not have you suffer such things."

She felt her world whirling about her. She knew she could not change his mind. For lack of a kindred and a bit of land they two must go separate and alone through all the dreary future. There must be something they could do. There must be. "My kin will be your kin, Bran," she said. "That we know. Carodoc will stand at your back and Abiris . . ." Her voice trailed off, seeing he was unmoved.

He beat his hands together and his voice was a wail of despair. "If I had but half a furlong of land and that covered with tares or lying in the midst of thick forest and you beside me, I would wrest from it all that we need."

A bit of land. To be separated by nothing more than that. There was land enough for all in the village holdings, even though much of it would need to be cleared. There must be a way to get some of it for Bran. Abiris could . . . Abiris *would* help. If he spoke to the headman of the tribe, there would be land for Bran, for a Druid's word was law. "Where is Abiris?" she asked.

Bran gaped at her. "Abiris? He is likely still upon the place of judgment with Carodoc and many others. Or was when I left him. Why?"

She did not answer him. She did not want to raise hopes that might be dashed again. "Will you wait here a little?" she asked. "I must see Abiris."

He nodded, wondering, but too miserable to ask more questions. She kissed the top of his head where his tonsure had been and went from him.

She was back again—before the water clock had marked half an hour—with a piece of birchbark, which she handed to Bran. He read it, listlessly at first, then with quickening excitement.

"It says"—he sounded bewildered—"it says that in—in consideration of the wrong done me and in—in recognition of obligation because of it—the—the tribe will grant me—two furlongs of good land in the forest—three leagues from the village in the lake—to be mine forever. And it says this land —this land shall belong to my—my heirs—unto all generations." He looked up at her, his eyes puzzled. "How, Ysobel? How comes this? The tribe does not easily surrender land to kin-shattered men. By what magic did you secure this writing?"

"Not I, Bran. Abiris. Abiris spoke to the headman of the tribe, spoke right willingly, for he would do anything in his power to set right the wrong done you."

"Abiris," Bran said slowly. "It must have brought him pain to believe me false. The old ways—the old ways are cruel, but Abiris knows no other. He had to abide by his own truth even though it hurt him sore." He was, a little, silent and she waited, knowing he had not yet done, feeling at last at one with him and at peace, content to wait. "Forgetting will not be so hard or so long," he whispered at last. "Who am I that I should judge another's truth, knowing so little of my own?"

She waited a moment more, and when he did not go on, she put her hand on his. "Bran. Abiris and Carodoc await us. Carodoc has your harp."

"My harp!" he shouted, and a great gladness came into

his face. "How I have missed it!" He caught her and lifted her until her head touched the top of the pavilion and swung her once and set her down and kissed her. He laughed aloud and was suddenly serious. "It will be hard, Ysobel. Hard to clear the land and bring a crop to harvest. We may know hunger, my birdling, and weariness and even sickness before we are done. Are you sure we would not best wait a little?"

"We have waited too long already, Bran, and I am done with it."

"Come, then." He put his arm about her shoulders. "Let us go to Abiris and Carodoc and before them declare our troth. And tomorrow we will seek our land together."

He led her from the pavilion, and together they walked beneath the star-filled sky toward the place where Abiris and Carodoc waited for them.

G34